Farewell, Cowboy

OLJA SAVIČEVIĆ

FAREWELL, COWBOY

Translated from the Croatian by Celia Hawkesworth

First published in 2015 by
Istros Books
London, United Kingdom www.istrosbooks.com

Originally published in Croatian as *Adio kauboju*

© Olja Savičević Ivančević, 2010

The right of Olja Savičević Ivančević to be identified as the author of this work has been asserted in accordance with the Copyright, Designs and Patents Act, 1988

Translation © Celia Hawkesworth, 2015

Graphic design: Davor Pukljak, Frontispis.hr

ISBN: 978-1-908236-48-7

Printed in England by
CMP (UK), Poole, Dorset | www.cmp-uk.com

Education and Culture DG

Culture Programme

This project has been funded with support from the European Commission. This publication reflects the views only of the author, and the Commission cannot be held responsible for any use which may be made of the information contained therein.

Eastern

STRANGER, THE LAW DOES NOT PROTECT YOU HERE

(Graffito, Main Jetty, Split, Croatia)

1

Summer 2009 came too early. This meant that ferocious heat had been building up ever since the beginning of May: the spring roses were expiring in the parks and stone troughs.

At the end of July I packed all my belongings, abandoned the borrowed apartment where I had lived through several lost years and set off for home.

My sister met me in the kitchen of our old house, with her suitcase already prepared for her departure. During our conversation lasting an hour and a half, she got up from the table four times, once to pour me some milk, and three times to go to the bathroom. Finally she came back with her lips coloured bright pink, which surprised me, but I didn't say anything. She hadn't used that colour lipstick before. While she was talking to me, she sent several text messages, and then finally she stood up, straightened her skirt and set off along the lengthy corridor and down the stairs. Ma was lying in her room on the lower floor, surfing channels.

They said goodbye briefly, at the front door, I heard their voices, and I watched from the balcony as my sister disappeared round the corner, behind the baker's house. For a moment she was an unreal apparition in a real scene, a simulation. I finished the cold coffee, in her cup with its smudge of pink lipstick.

Before she vanished, my sister had told me something of her daily ritual with Ma over the past month. It was precise and simple: they rose early, always at the same time, and spent at least twenty minutes over coffee. Then, before the sun was too hot, they set off on foot, one behind the other, along the main road to the cemetery. In summer, the thin strip of earth beside the road, barely wide enough for two narrow feet, turned to dust. Between the road on one side and the brambles, groundsel and unplastered houses on the other side of an imagined pavement, dust rose up, getting into your eyes and throat and between your toes in your sandals.

'D'you know some folks eats earth?' my sister asked my mother as they trudged through the dust, beside the main road. 'It's called "geophagy".'

But Ma responded tangentially, as she so often did these days: 'Dust to dust, better be buried in earth than immured in concrete.'

'Death don't bother me none,' my sister broke in. 'Fuck death. You can get used to it too, I'm sure.'

''Course it don't bother you,' Ma was offended. She shook the dust out of her clog and strode on, chin in the air, with all the dignity of a future deceased person, one step ahead of my sister.

After they had washed *our* grave and cut the rotted stalks off the flowers, they would make their way down to the beach with a more-sprightly step.

'It's calm and quiet as a microwave,' my sister had remarked as they passed through other people's gardens and desiccated orchards.

At the beach, Ma took squashed pears and bananas out of the paper bag in a plastic bag in a Tupperware box, and offered them, with her famous Hollywood smile (which ought to make any normal person feel a bit better, observed my sister). But she thought Ma used to just pluck that expression out of a folder or the big straw basket she toted around wherever she went. And it seemed to her that sometimes Ma would produce that smile, the ace from a sleeve of mass-produced expressions, at the wrong moment.

Their togetherness would come to an end with their return home, after lunch, when my sister would withdraw to her room upstairs, till supper time, and try to get on with her own work, even though she was on holiday (she's a school teacher). Ma would then feed ginger Jill, settle down in front of the television and announce: 'My serial's starting.'

Minerva, Aaron and Isadora had decided to investigate the true identity of Vasiona Morales. She was a very dangerous woman who had to be separated from Juan.

In Ma's eyes all serials are important, and equally so.

She would fall asleep in front of the TV, wrapped up to her ears, although at the time the temperature didn't fall below 30 even at night.

The day I left Zagreb, my sister told me she was terrified that Ma was going to overdo her sleeping pills – she didn't stir under the sheet, she didn't even breathe, just occasionally farted in her sleep.

'She's dreadful,' Ma said of my sister after she'd left. 'She says terrible things. I don't get it, Dada.' That's what I'm called – Dada, that's the name my parents gave me.

When I accompany Ma to the highway, the heat rises from the earth: by seven it's up to one's ankles. On dry mornings, just after midday, it starts grilling down straight from the sky. In town it's worst around five pm – the salt air begins to sweat and everything that moves passes limply through treacle, while the song-of-a-million sounds is transformed into a steady, electric hum that hypnotizes.

Although she's perfectly upright when she sits or stands, when she's walking Ma rolls over the edges of a line. Cisterns and refrigerated-fish lorries hurtle past a few centimetres from her shoulder. Maybe there's just no place any more for a non-driver in traffic, I reflect.

'They should be shut up in pedestrian gulags, those idiots don't realize their life's on the line,' my sister said once, I think it was when we were driving in her ex-husband's turbo off-roader to Daniel's funeral, and some kids suddenly tore across the road.

'Pedestrians have to be loved. Pedestrians created the world. And when it was all done, cars appeared,' I said. Everyone looked at me as though I was nuts. 'It says that in a book somewhere,' I added.

I was sitting in the back on sticky, fake leather, surrounded by wreaths of palm branches that pricked my bare arms, among arrangements of chrysanthemums and bunches of blousy roses with big red ribbons. The wreaths had mauve ribbons and names written in gold felt-tip.

'So folks knows who's sorry,' my sister remarked, which was deemed inappropriate.

'My, but we's primitive,' she then added, closing the window out of which she had tossed a still-lit butt the colour of blood, 'things like this proves it. Every love's weighed, see, the bigger the death notice, the bigger the advertisement, the more marble on the grave or gold on the cross. More cash, more love. Chucking money around. The more luxurious the vacuum cleaner he gives the young couple, the bigger the brother's love, 's all the same. There's no such thing as a poor relation, just a tight-fisted sod who doesn't love you,' she turned to tell me.

I was sweltering among the prickly wreaths, trying not to crush the flowers and watching people picking cherries beside the cement works. They had ladders, caps and blue aprons. They looked contented in their manual toiling. I wondered whether cement dust scattered over them as they pulled down the branches with their long-handled pincers. I remembered that dust as being like a soft carpet; it was an agreeable memory.

I didn't answer my sister and that provoked her to keep on talking, sentences that flew like projectiles round the absence of my reply. Her former husband, a peaceable and transparent type, soft and stiff, said: 'OK, calm down, now.'

As we walk along the side of the motorway, my mother is transformed into a mole alongside a poster of a pastoral centre on which is written *Jesus Loves You*, then into an extinguished glow-worm beside the discount store and into a minus sign when moving beneath a larger-than-life-sized, washed-out poster of our very own 'Hero not War Criminal,' General Gotovina. We walk on in the dust beside the road by the petrol station, on a path barely wide enough for two narrow feet. The speed limit here is sixty, but people drive at least eighty and a little further on, the four-lane fast road comes to an end and drivers lose all sense of speed. Farmers in their tractors are known to come out onto the highway from one of the unmade-up side lanes and slow the traffic down to a crawl.

Until recently there was also horse shit on the highway, but not any more. It's become too dangerous to drive a cart and horses there. And I think there's just one man in the whole town with a horse now; it's illegal to keep a horse in town now, but he's the old blacksmith, and they're just waiting for him to die in peace, if Ma is to be believed. What'll happen to that horse, when the blacksmith dies, I wonder. There used to be a smithy in the Old Settlement run by that old man, in the port where the restaurant *La Vida Loca* is now. But it closed the year Daniel was born. I remember the sound of the shoeing, the horses neighing at the darkness and fire. I was still very small, and I looked at things from a distance, staring out of the summer light that hurts the eyes, into the open darkness of that building. I was still very small when along the street where we lived one would hear hoof beats on the worn stone, an unreal sound the way the sound of a Ledo van inviting you to have an ice cream during the afternoon siesta is unreal. Willy Wonka has come to your town too.

But there are no longer fresh horse-droppings in the streets. Dogs shit and no one picks up after them, just as they didn't after the horses. But no one's going to throw dog turds at you, you can be sure. That really would surprise me.

When the shape of my mother in the distance becomes a line – a horizontal line, a minus, rather than vertical, as one might have expect, because of the glare on the road, I turn and hurry towards the house, along the concrete stream beside the new buildings for disabled veterans. There used to be all kinds of rubbish and treasure in that stream: in springtime it would hurl itself over the trash barrier. Since it's been cleaned out and lined with concrete, I've noticed that a ribbon of slime trickles along it, congealing into green mud in summer.

'You could go to the cemetery on your own tomorrow,' I suggested to Ma the day after I arrived. 'I've got things to do in town, it's quite important,' I lied.

Ma smiled at that, exactly as my sister had said she would, producing her Hollywood smile at the wrong moment. She had nice teeth, a gold incisor in her lower jaw. Sometimes she would tap her teeth with her fingernail to demonstrate their firmness and health.

'Mother looks like a smiley on speed,' I told my sister over the phone, later.

'See what I mean,' she replied, blowing smoke into the receiver at her end.

I tell her I found Xanax, some Prozac, Diazepam, Praxiten and Valium on the floor, under the dresser in the kitchen, in an ancient, boiled-sweet tin, along with plasters, Aspirin and cough pastilles. Ma wasn't even hiding them, as my sister had presumed – or else Ma knew that one of the best places to hide things is where they can be seen. Yet last winter she had thrown them all into the bin, I saw her do it.

'Where on earth does she get them?' asked my sister, incensed.

It's not hard, I thought. Half the student hostel was on vodka or wine combined with Valium, sedatives and other bits and pieces that can theoretically only be got on prescription. They're cheaper than sweets.

'Leave her some Lorsilan to help her sleep,' my sister advised. 'Anything else you finds you can chuck down the toilet.' I flushed it several times, but one blue Prozac capsule kept floating back to the surface. In the end, though, even that persistent one disappeared.

Later, as I sit on the swing on our balcony, I can see out over the roofs. Our neighbours greet me from the street and I wave back.

When Ma appears – first a minus sign, then a mole – from the west, behind the baker's house, I wave to her too. As soon as she reaches the door, I tell her: 'I've decided to stay for a while, Ma. Could you take Daniel's things out of my cupboard?'

She's standing in the cloakroom, in front of the washbasin, rubbing soap into her hands under a jet of water.

'Yes,' she says, turning off the water, drying her hands with a stiff towel.

'There's no point taking flowers in summer, they all burns up in a day,' she adds thoughtfully.

'I'll use the rebate on my pension,' says Ma later, dividing the melon with a blunt knife as we sit in the hybrid dining/living room we call the tunnel. 'To fix up the grave.' She says she'll put the shares she's sold into my account. 'You never know, one day you might want to finish your degree.'

I say: 'OK. But I'll keep it for my own pension, by then folk'll be able to go to the moon. Although your shares won't be enough for even two minutes on the moon.'

At least you'll be able to go to the moon,' she concludes thoughtfully and, nodding, she drags her slippers behind the green curtain that divides the kitchen from the improvized room.

'You's hungry,' the green curtain shouts now. 'But there's no fresh bread. I couldn't get none, the Albanian closed early. Give me a moment, I'll make some French toast.'

I don't like French toast, I begin to say, why can't you remember, but I change my mind and say: 'Fine.'

Behind the curtain I hear the clink of tin plates and eggs being broken, milk gurgling.

'Did you know that swallow-fish moult when they come back south from the north. Their feathers fall out, and they grow scales and fins so they can swim again.'

I sometimes tell her idiocies like this to amuse myself.

'Everything's possible after Chernobyl,' she replies, beating the egg yolk, milk and sugar together briskly. 'The Mišković woman from Lower Street gave birth to one child with three fathers.'

My room is a box in a house of boxes.

At a time I don't remember, this was a cellar full of barrels, then it was used as a larder, so there are no windows in the room. Just a narrow door, a narrow table, a huge wardrobe, with a large Crying Baby Doll on top of it, and a bed, with a few of Daniel's left-over ancient film posters on the walls, mostly Westerns. There's a dry olive twig tucked behind one of them, in memory of John Wayne.

Before it was Daniel's room, and before it was mine, that catacomb on the ground floor, in the depths of the house, was where my mother's gran had lived, motionless, a blind and immobile diabetic. Five years in the dark, without moving, entirely conscious.

'Santo Subito', said my aunts and some women whose particular faces under their permanent waves I can't remember. There was one blind woman who never protested or complained much, which is a sound reference for sainthood. She recited her prayers with thin lips that had once been full. In the old photographs of our grandmother my sister noticed the same thing: 'A smoker's lips,' she remarked, grinning.

There was nothing that ancient woman would rather talk about than love, with a lot of spice. As we grew up and she began to fade, the old lady's youth became ever more unbridled, until in the end – in our recollection of her past – she was canonized as *the insatiable one.*

She buried three husbands, gave birth to five children and in her mature womanly days she was able to scythe a field of brambles, fennel and asparagus – so it was said – and then eat two kilos of shellfish for lunch and wash them down with three quarters of a litre of red – so it was said. She swore out loud and frequently and prayed with equal fervour.

Throughout her stay with us, Mother systematically disinfected the little room, I remember. There were mothballs in all the cupboards, the odour of lavender and camphor in the corners.

'She's afraid the old girl's going to fall to pieces on her, any minute now she'll be dousing her in formalin,' said my sister. 'Or quicklime.'

The embalmed old lady, fairly emaciated, was not much bigger than me or Daniel then. She was vanishing before our eyes, day by day, on her high bed, with heaps of quilts, from under which she squeaked: 'Children! Oh, children!'

My sister and I sometimes pretended not to hear her, I remember, but Daniel was something else, it didn't bore him.

There's a song from those days that Ma often sang around the house:

You're a heavenly flower
Beloved by all each hour
You are the one I love
All others far above
And she went out alone, not a word to her mother
To pluck roses for her dearest lover...

Later I sang that song to Daniel, and Daniel sang it to our great-grandmother while she lay with her open, watery eyes in *eternal darkness*.

'Hey, Gran, do you see everything in black and white, like hell?' he asked her.

'Hell's no black, hell's green, and shiny with plankton. Inside me too's all green, like a Martian's bum.'

Daniel used to press his eyes deep into his skull, I recall.

'Then your eyes turn over and you see inside, into yourself,' he said.

He pressed his eyes until he began to feel sick, yet he didn't, as far as I know, see a yellowy-green light. He didn't see that until later, one summer when the sea blossomed with seaweed full of phosphorus. During the day it looked like a puddle of dung, *mare sporco*, but at night every movement we made would scatter into fluorescent bubbles.

'And heaven?'

'Heaven? There be no heaven. Aah. Just hell, right here, on the black earth!' the old lady moaned in pain. Then she added: 'O, santo dio Benedetto, holy shit. Come, come, my little dove, sing that *Not a word to her mother*.'

A few days before our great-grandmother's death a little monkey that lived at the time in our neighbour the vet's garden, slipped into our house. People said some rich tourists had grown bored with it and left it behind. It caused havoc all over the house, that monkey. We spent ages looking for it, I recall, it had crept in under the old lady's oversized nightdress. Sneaky beast, we said. And soon it escaped the vet altogether, first into the park, and then who knows where.

'Does yous love Great-Granny?' asked my sister.

Daniel and I nodded. The old lady was our wooden reptile – she touched our cheeks with her dry, odourless antennae. Our underground doll from the attic.

'Then we's got to help her,' said my sister, her green eyes looking at us straight from hell.

'Great-Granny's suffering,' she said, 'and we's got to help her fly up to heaven'.

I believe she really thought that. That we'd put a pillow over her head. a child playing with weapons is a terrible thing, and everything is a weapon, I recall. It's really amazing that so many of us have survived our own and other people's childhoods.

'Heaven don't exist,' said Daniel quickly. 'Go ask her.'

Things were easier with Daniel. That was the end of it.

'Don't let Ma hear yous,' I whispered.

'I never said God don't exist.'

'You's idiots! Pathetic! And craven,' said my sister. Her contempt was terrible, I recall. Still is, for that matter.

Craven, where'd she got that word from? Some film, I imagine.

And the old lady – 'poor thing, poor thing' everyone said – really did cry out for help and blaspheme against God and the devil.

I think my sister loved Great-Granny, though you never know with her.

She prayed fervently to the saints for the old lady to die, even at mealtimes, which earned her a smack.

In the end her passionate spiritual euthanasia worked.

Great-Granny died like a fish, her mouth open.

That was the first time we'd seen death–it didn't look that terrible.

She was lying on her bed, with her eyes finally closed and Daniel lifted up her wide nightdress dating from the time when she was *the insatiable one*. We were looking for the tourists' monkey, but there was nothing under her nightdress. Everything about Great-Granny had been dead for years already, her blue and brown shanks covered in scabs, hairless. The only thing alive was the muff between her legs, shaggy, shiny fur, bright black, that climbed from half-way up her thighs to her groin and then in a narrow spindle up to her belly button.

'Is that the monkey?' I asked.

'A cat,' said Daniel, surprised, covering her up with the nightdress.

That evening I discovered a hair under my panties. One single hair, but I couldn't pull it out. I was almost a boy, just like my brother, who was 'like a little girl' my aunts used to say.

That wasn't right, though, because Daniel was a boy the way boys are like those carved wooden angels that are supposed to guard your house or those Gothic ones with cheery expressions. They are free from either male or female sins, the only sunny, full-blooded creatures in church frescoes or in free flight above anorexic saints, hysterics and virgins in the side aisles. Perhaps that's because they have interesting jobs to do, dealing with the profane interactions between demigods and people.

The chubby little gilded angel above the Pietà behind the altar in St Fjoko's Church still chuckles at me today, sucking his thumb or picking his nose. All the devout ladies dream of nibbling his cheeks.

A neglected angel, perhaps, but not from a porcelain cup and not a little girl – that was our Daniel.

My room is a box in a house of boxes. Above the room there's a bathroom, so damp stains come through the fresh paint on the ceiling. The bed behind the low cupboard is a still smaller box. The next box is me. The smallest box, a boxlet, is my cunt.

Before I go to sleep, I put each little box into the next, and then in the last one I put everything it's agreeable to think about, everything that soothes me. Such as going into a clean empty kitchen, in which the fridge is purring, the sound of an aeroplane landing or taking off, something warm with a neutral smell like a dry child's or cat's head, sniffing the tips of one's fingers, the chance touch of strangers, unexpected, with no ulterior motive; a hallucination while perfectly rational – that I am the white contents of a capsule or yoghurt being poured out in a single dollop.

But if I spend too long awake, with insomnia that becomes like delirium and a torment, images appear, bursting rapidly into leaf.

The images I see most frequently are shots from an amateur porn video taken off the Internet, which I came across at a party two or three years ago. The images have rooted in my consciousness, draining and annoying me, because particularly nauseating images have a way of keep coming back and not fading. It was a custom at certain gatherings to show such amateur little films in one of the rooms, in the small hours, films that had been allegedly taken from certain sites, nothing illegal, allegedly, although I wouldn't swear to it. The party guests would try to make fun of the two, three or five people sporting lively genitals on the screen. I would most often wander out of the room at the very beginning of the projection, but this time I stayed to the end, because the main actor's face caught my attention.

The film was poor quality and too dark, it had evidently been dark in the room where it was made. It was probably shot with a mobile, I thought at the time.

It begins with the expression on the face of a man rearing up over a thin, white body. The man doing the fucking has very large hands and his face, which I can't make out clearly, is blurred, but it seems to be on the verge of tears. The person under him occasionally moves an arm or leg and emits a barely audible moaning sound. Then there's a cut and the next image is of the narrow thighs of that second person, boy or girl, it's hard to tell: the thighs are bare and pressed together, with a thin barb between them, the big man's snout. The third scene shows a boyish nape, with short hair and a huge fat hand on it: the face of the person being fucked by the big man is hidden by a pillow and can't be seen. The fourth scene moves, but barely: with one hand the fucker holds the object of his lust by the shoulder or neck, probably too tightly, and slowly pushes it downwards, grabs it lower down, thrusting in and ramming slowly and powerfully and crying increasingly loudly, then coming with a roar and a wail. His crying is the thing it's impossible to forget, particularly if you want to.

I wouldn't be able to say that these scenes excite me; rather they disturb me. There are some images that bruise me like slaps on the face: such as those of that huge ejaculating, crying man whose face I can't put together.

In my box of boxes, droplets of sweat travel down my ribs, I stop them with the tips of my fingers and rub them over my belly. I turn the pillow onto its dry side, push my hands down inside my panties between my thighs and try to curl up towards the aroma between my legs. That used to send me to sleep when I was a child.

Finally, I give up on my efforts to fall asleep, I take off my damp t-shirt and light a cigarette sitting by the low window of the summer kitchen, looking up into the blue cleft above the street from where, instead of the freshness of nocturnal dew, a moist, lukewarm blancmange is sliding over the town.

All that can be heard in the Settlement is snoring – interrupted by curses and squeaking springs, the irritated thrashing of limbs coming through holes in the neighbouring houses – and a cat exhaling air through its tiny nostrils. Someone's left a player on and it's emitting a thin repetitive squeak. The fat town is sleeping in a fever, the guttersnipe.

It's almost six, but the air outside is already warmer than inside.

Looking back, I can see clearly that everything had changed faster and more fundamentally than I had. I must have spent the last few years standing still on a conveyor belt, while everything else was rushing and growing. I rarely came home, caught off-guard every time I went to the centre, to the west end of the town, where my sister lives, into that scintillating showroom, that garish shop-window of a broken and robbed world. Going into town is a digital adventure in which I'm met round familiar corners by ever newer and more unrestrained silicon hordes. The adrenalin scattered through the air is an aerosol that fills and pierces my lungs.

I go to the big beaches with their concrete plateaux, recliners and cocktail bars, to the marinas, where there are Russian yachts larger than our houses and to hotel complexes with ramps and a caretaker; a mass of rubble and broken glass, diggers and trucks, steel scaffolding, and smooth prisms of black opaque glass whose metal glare assaults your vision. But I pity only the birds, the dolphins and flying fish. I believe that these things must horrify them when they leap out of the water or fly down from the sky.

In the east is the industrial zone. The east is a great stranded wreck. The shipyard with its tall green cranes, hangars, cement factories and abandoned railway tracks, and behind that vast garbage heap, on the edge of a peninsula, is the shabby Old Settlement, with a post office and church and dark runny mud in the polluted port, a comical little place under the distant skyscrapers, which blink at night at us beneath them...At me and Ma sitting on the balcony, sipping tepid beer out of plastic bottles or eating melon, while a fan on the railing pretends to be a breeze. Our neighbours who don't have air-conditioning sleep on settees dragged out onto the terrace; whole families. Around the evening news time they sit round and watch TV. Here, nothing has changed; it hasn't budged. Perhaps this is the only corner of the world I know, my haven, my salvation, my place of greater safety. Despair and refuge, a shred of happiness in a lukewarm bitter liquid.

The oleanders, capers and bougainvilleas have come into flower in the courtyards. And our cat, ginger Jill, has a street light like a star in each eye.

On such evenings the world and the town are not divided into east and west, but, as in an animal's head, simply into north and south. Because that, *urbi et orbi*, is the language of moss, compasses and wind roses, migrating birds, the rhythms by which people rise and dance, the kinetic language that divides into hemispheres; eels and smelts that mate ecstatically in the shallows, so that you can tread among them, through that lively seething and flickering, migrating birds, *mapa mundi*, Luna and the North Star and the place up on the hill up to where the broom bushes grow.

Ah, that's when everything seems to be OK, and sometimes that's the same as if it was.

Back here, I know every rat-run, hiding place and way out in case of danger.

As kids we all had that knowledge – in our legs more than in our heads, like a foreign language that waited, rolling around in our middle ear, whose hot-blooded Romance melody we had woven into our own, far more languid Slav one. Me, my sister and Daniel, and the boys too, who came to us from the new estates beyond the railway – the Iroquois Brothers' family and some other outlanders, always with freshly shaved heads in summer. At that time they wanted to be like us, so they gabbled the way we did, differently from their sweet fat mums and hairy dads whose consonants stuck in their gullets and who used to yell, whenever they needed to speak.

We cobbled that language together from what we learned at home from our parents as much as from the unknown translators of film subtitles and dubbed cartoons; the language we'd picked up in the street and from announcers on the News and stolen from Dylan Dog, Grunf, Sammy Jo Carrington and Zane Grey. It was the musical *lingua franca* from the west of the city and the centre through the Old Settlement and as far as the railway. Wherever there were kids who talked and called to one another. We sought each other out and hung out, there was nothing else to do, and nor did there need to be.

Variations on the game of hide-and-seek offered endless possibilities. Or the game of *group seeks group*. Back alleys lead through unlocked villas, or through the kitchen of the cake shop with big vats of custard and tubs of ice cream, through dark vaults leading down to still darker cellars. The cellars come to an end in tight passages between buildings, pipes that emerge into bare courtyards with sheets drying above them, steps that end in the sky, garrets on rotten beams, roofs over which we leap to the old castle, then we clamber up on the sea side, dragging ourselves along the edge of the wall, and coming down into the park, under upturned boats in dry berths.

That's where we found Daniel, the first time he got lost; he had hidden under a boat on the slipway during a game of hide-and-seek and sung to himself so as not to be afraid. After that he kept disappearing and he would stay away for increasingly long spells – because he was no longer afraid, he said.

We thought all our games and wars must be even more exciting than those of the children who grew up in the movies with the cactuses and the big bright sun over the wide prairie. After all, there is a prairie here, too, at the foot of the hill above the cemetery where my father and brother are buried, even though now the path there is cut off by huge houses with hens pecking around them.

It was in a battle on the lunar expanse behind the cement works and old saltpans, between the road and the prairie, that I won my real name, Rusty, because of my red hair. That day I fell three times for justice and liberty, I was a courageous general and that's the name I call myself – Rusty – in private.

Immediately after the war, through an exchange of volunteers, a precocious first-year student from Heidelberg ended up among us. He had come to interview us for their student radio station about the post-war life of young people in Croatia.

'You live in a multicultural country...' he began.

'No, I don't,' I said into the dictaphone, distinctly, as though it was a microphone.

'Oh, I knows what he means,' my sister butted in. 'There's various nations here, at least two nations in every house in our street, but it's all the same mangy culture, if you asks me. Only the Chinese can save us from boredom.'

My sister had her own way of being imbued with the spirit of internationalism.

'Eh,' said my sister to the lad from Heidelberg, slapping him on the shoulder in a comradely way, 'before this war we used to play at war with the tourists; then the little Germans and Italians acted Germans and Italians. '

'And in this war? And afterwards?' he cleared his throat and turned the dictaphone towards me.

'Oh, I don't know. No one played at these Balkan wars, if that's what you mean. Fuck it, they all wanted to be Croats.'

'Yep,' my sister confirmed.

'That's why we played cowboys and Indians.'

'With the outlanders.'

'Against the outlanders. You have to have some kind of conflict: cowboys and Indians.'

English and Dutch people had recently settled in our narrow lane, followed by Belgians and French people – I don't think the Chinese believe that poverty is especially romantic. It was fascinating to watch dwellings stuck together with stone, cement and bird droppings, with worms burrowing through their beams and mice nesting in them, turn into little picture-book cottages. It was a delight for those with a bit of time and money.

All the Chinese people I've ever met live in high-rise blocks, I reflected. There are those who value the solidity of construction,

I completely get that. They are people who live in settlements like ours all over the world.

'Jesus, these tourists are cracked,' said my sister before taking her suitcase and going down the hall, saying goodbye to us and disappearing behind the baker's house, leaving a greasy, pinkish mark on her cup. My sister calls all the westerners who have moved into our street over the last few years, transforming those hovels into pleasant summer-houses, tourists.

'Paint away, carry on painting,' she said, watching our Irish neighbour waving to us in a friendly way from under a paper cap. 'You'll never get rid of the damp and woodworm, the stink of burned onions, or the kids on your steps.'

Perhaps that's why they come, I thought.

The daddy tourists push their children around in buggies, and we see them hanging out washing on the line between houses in the street. They don't grill fish on charcoal in an old concrete mould or cardboard box in front of their front door with the other men in blue overalls. And they haven't learned to play cards.

We used to have my father's Yugoslav National Army officers, but they all married *nice* girls and evaporated after a while during the last war, or they ran off after some skirt, and their wives went back to their parents' kitchens, in their unsuitably fine dresses, and later concealed their children's surnames. We also used to have the working fathers, manual workers, usually from Macedonian or, more often, Bosnian villages, who married *bad* girls. They stayed on in our street, to drink with their wives and fight with their sons. Or the other way round. They were the only fathers we ever saw, apart from the occasional sailor or a dad working abroad. Every time they came home, those men would find a new bun in the oven.

And then there was my father, not quite like anyone else. He bore the surname of his long-dead mother, and whether his old man had been a Kraut, as people said, no one knew for sure. At home no one talked about that, he least of all. He had this red hair and light skin. Like me and Daniel.

My sister is the image of Mother, she looks like the other women in the Old Settlement: brown velvet, black silk, sandpaper.

Later Daniel transformed that unknown forebear into a soldier of the Third Reich who falls in love with a young virgin in the occupied Town from – to make matters worse, but more interesting – a Partisan family. He returns several years after the war and in a brief and passionate affair he gives her a son. They never see each other again; she dies young of grief, a victim of complex political circumstances.

I believe that my father heard this story, because one morning at breakfast, out of the blue, he said that his phantom old man had been a customs officer from Cetinje.

'Well honestly,' said my sister later. 'Whoever heard of a red-haired Montenegrin?!'

'Our old man is an incredible loser,' she added. This was the time when older boys were beginning to smoke Croatian cigarettes, war was just brewing and everyone had suddenly become nationally aware. 'He's always on the wrong side. First he was a Kraut, and now he's a Montenegrin.' Montenegrins were historically aligned with Serbs, and that was the wrong side to us.

'Filthy half-breed!' said Tommy Iroquois to Daniel in the course of one of our fights, belching like a pig.

'Lousy redskin! Scabby Indian!' responded Daniel, belching even more loudly and piggily, and knocking him into the dust.

A half-breed like Castellari's Keoma, like McQueen's Nevada Smith. Or Sergio Leone's Nobody.

On several occasions, the neighbour with whom we quarrelled about the communal steps cursed our Kraut mother. We used to curse her cunning, heathen mother in a familiar manner. But in principle, we never knew who was what, so we were caught off guard when everyone else knew who we were better than we did. The advent of the war had a way of making people's ethnicity everybody's business.

It still happens today that one neighbour will spit on another or piss on his car tyres or pour dirty water over his children during their afternoon siesta. Sometimes the women, who are more highly strung here and fiercer than their weary husbands, fight so that their tits gleam and their teeth and kitchen knives flash. But, this pathetic neighbourhood is no worse than others when you grow up in it – that's what I think when I sit with Ma on the balcony and we drink beer from plastic bottles, and the fan pretends to be wind. When the night's sultry, those neighbours who don't go off to bathe with a towel slung over their shoulders, amuse themselves singing outside their houses.

And I join in, whispering, from my bed: *You're a heavenly flower*.

This business with the cowboys was my father's doing. He started it, and somehow it was his story. Everyone else in Yugoslavia liked the Indians best, apparently because of our most popular TV series, which had Winnetou, the Indian boy as the hero. It was only much later that cowboys came into their own. But my father loved the proper cowboys: John Ford, Zinnemann, he used to say. He adored the Italian westerns of Leone and Sergio Corbucci, he said he liked Sam Fucking Peckinpah as well and all the films acted in and directed by 'the great Ned Montgomery', as he called him. Since he became my late father, I have dreamed about him twice, the same dream both times. How it was before, when I was able to smell him after his morning shave, rubbing my cheek against his chin – of course I don't remember that, because then dreams were different. Ordinary dreams about other things.

In my dream, my father is coming towards me, accompanied by a bird. It is the same cockatoo that used to peck at the top of his ballpoint pen while he did Rebus and crossword puzzles in his leisure time in the afternoon. He took it everywhere, my father did. It cackled on his shoulder as he sat at a table on the waterfront with the other tall men from the settlement. The crested fashion-model strutted about, turned her idiotic little chicken's head around self-importantly, crapped on the light fittings and cupboards and watched out for a chance to leap onto someone's head and peck their skull, I recall. It was only my father to whom she attached herself with some kind of servile avian devotion. Nothing like a hawk whose devotion, were it not so magnificent, would be canine, I thought. The cockatoo, as my sister described it, had the temperament of a monkey and the manners of a possessive little madam.

The parrot imitated the way our father whistled to call us in from the street, striking terror into our hearts, because our father was strict. Later he softened, as though he knew that he had no time for anything other than fun. In summer he took us to a distant sandy beach and to play badminton and brought us copies of the latest videocassettes of films and MTV clips and pulp fiction that we watched or read in the quiet, empty seasons. He kissed our feet and eyes and under our chins, where a child is softest.

Sometimes I spent winter mornings at the Little Lagoon looking for cuttlefish shells for the cockatoo, to please my father, and that bird of his, which no one in the house liked.

'You'll make great soup, you're just right for soup,' said Daniel. He threatened the bird from a respectable distance kissing the tips of his fingers and smacking his lips.

'It'd make a great crown of feathers,' he told me once quite seriously.

'Hey, you'd be a great headdress!' he shouted to the parrot.

Daniel thought that if an animal talks, it must also understand. And if I think about it, for that matter so did I, because once I said something to it and our cat Jill looked at me and sighed.

'Oh,' came a muffled sound that you often hear dogs make.

And Jill's just an exasperated dumb creature who reads our lips, but perhaps she does hear. She certainly feels our words but isn't capable of repeating or creating them, I thought. But still my words reach Jill like flying objects, invisible artefacts – when I say *food*, she hears the crisp rind of bacon with red strips of meat, when I say *love*, she hears my hand, its moistness and warmth, my pulse.

Although it was able to repeat them, our words reached the cockatoo as noises, simple melodies.

Our pa was taken ill early, so the guys from the cement works employed him in the factory cinema. The *Balkan Cinema* it was called back then. It's been closed for ages now.

He tore the tickets in half, stuck up posters, carried huge reels of film and showed the films along with Uncle Braco. Those were brilliant years for his children, the last years of that cinema, just before the war: three days a week. After the matinee I sat in the little projection room, with the projector whirring, leafing through catalogues of the films that would be coming or reading about those that would never be shown in our cinema.

After the screening, we would come out into a night full of stars pricked into the black, above the tubular, pot-bellied factory halls and chimneys painted red and white like a lollipop, and tread over the carpet of cement dust that stretched to the edge of the sea and beyond, far below the sea. Roundabout, in the dust, lay perfectly smooth metal globes, some small, some large, that were probably used for grinding marl, and steel rollers that we took to make go-karts, I recall.

We came out of the old *Balkan Cinema* – hearing the wooden seats clatter as they folded up behind us – as though we were passing from one film into another.

And as a finale: the spongy, muffled sound of the large cinema door closing, then my father turning the key and putting it away in the inner pocket of his jacket like the keeper of a secret.

I was proud of him then, far more proud than if he'd been a doctor, a singer or a director.

After that Uncle Braco opened a video rental shop, *Braco & Co.*, where my father was the *Co.* until the end of his short life, working behind the counter.

I asked him whether we were going to have our own video shop.

'What'll it be called?' I asked, pushing myself into his hands.

'It'll be called *Almeria*,' he said, tracing the invisible name in the air with his finger and winking.

My excitement in those years sprang from a different world but continued in this one, equally exciting.

A life lasting a whole evening, a film lasting a whole life in which the best heroes lived just long enough to act an episode, for you to like them.

In my dream, my father coughs, just as he did in real life. His lungs are overgrown with little silver asbestos hairs, which you can clearly see through him. You can see through him everything it's essential to see, only it's hard to reproduce it when you're awake.

'Eh, where've you sprung from?' I ask him in that dream, in which he appears in the company of the bird.

He smiles, draws from a phantom holster, winks and says: 'Bang, bang!'

'Bang, bang!' repeats the parrot from his shoulder. 'Bang, bang!'

Ma and I didn't talk about the dope, or its mysterious disappearance from the tin under the dresser. Which wasn't that mysterious, after all. And what was there to be said, after all. As though it was possible to drive the devil out, one has to sit down beside one's demon and mollify it until it's calm – that's all, perhaps, that can be done.

From time to time Ma seemed agitated – for instance, she dropped things. But that used to happen before as well. Once it seemed to me that she reeked of alcohol.

Otherwise, she watched TV or swept the pavement in front of the house in the evening, to get some air. She would sprinkle the street with water that evaporated before it was swallowed by the manholes.

We didn't even cook, although Ma is a cook, or used to be. Mostly we ate meals from the *foodshop*, ordered on the free number 0800 30 33 01. They offered heated-up frozen things that the workers bought cheaply at the nearby market and threw into hot oil in a wok.

The menu included bizarre hogwash such as veal medallions in tuna sauce, *wtf*... But I don't care, I'm perfectly happy with a plastic plate containing meat and rice, if possible not stuck together, and beet-root salad, and there isn't even any washing up, it doesn't taste of anything and it's all consumed without exaggerated emotion about food. Sometimes they add a little vacuum-packed chocolate cake.

This morning she got up very early, I recognized the sound of the vacuum cleaner. She had taken out all her shoes, new, old and those that no one wore any longer, and arranged them on the steps. I found her brushing them and rubbing polish into them.

My coffee was getting cold and there was a short, sharp hair in it. Jill had probably licked it, the wicked cat. I took the hair out with my finger and drank.

As soon as she saw me through the open front door, Ma abandoned her shoe brush and ran up, wiping her hands on a rag as she came. As though she'd hardly been able to wait for me to wake up.

'Look, I wanted to show you this,' she said excitedly. 'What do you think? Is it tacky?'

On a shiny piece of paper was written:

GERBERA HEART (code: 3-70606)
Pain, sorrow and melancholy are part of life, especially at the times when we remember our dearest ones who are no longer with us. This arrangement symbolizes two hearts, which will remain forever together. It is made up of red mini gerberas, red roses and seasonal greenery arranged in the form of a heart.
Dimensions: width 42 cm, height 40 cm.
PRICE: 425.50 kunas

The arrangement in the picture looked like a strawberry cream gateau.

Her glasses had slipped to the tip of her nose, an old-fashioned frame, comical.

'It's not too tacky, is it?'

'It's lovely,' I said.

Outside we were met by a mass-produced dry morning, where everything was burnt-up: the sky that had lost its colour and the two of us, without a drop of blood, were trudging along the uneven road beside the stream towards the highway. I have a new straw hat, yellow, on the label it says it is in fact a hat made of paper. As I put it on, I think of Tom Waits in Down By Law, that is, his attitude to cowboy boots – when you walk that much, you surely like boots – or Puss-in-Boots, Supertramps and all those valiant warriors, lonely riders, walkers, their spurs and rivets, Pipi Long Stocking's enormous shoes and Henry Thoreau's philosophical hiking boots, the sandals of some young wanderer and especially those boots of Nancy Sinatra's, made for walking. Perhaps I would be able to develop such an attitude with this hat? I would certainly like to develop such an attitude towards the hat, which is not difficult when there is so much sun. I felt like telling someone about this, Daniel most likely.

Ma is dragging her beach things, for afterwards, she's shoved a linen cap adorned with some obscure logo over her eyes and steps out, while behind her, I'm expiring under the seasonal greenery of the Gerbera Heart. *Seasonal greenery*, that's what they call it, as though there was anything green in this season apart from inside greenhouses.

There is nothing green anywhere you look. Only dust and thorn bushes; needles and pins. My tongue is hard and my throat sprinkled with flour, the spring juices have now turned to dust and my blood has turned to dust, I'm sure that in males of all species their sperm has turned to dust. Perhaps they spurt it out like confetti or cannons of artificial snow. That thought amused me, for a moment.

I'm aware of my head swaying above the Gerbera Heart, above my bare legs, on the burning highway and I see Ma up ahead in the haze, scuttling along in her gold clogs.

If I could weep, I would probably weep tablets: milligram-sized. I recalled a story in which a girl wept roses, yellow ones, I think, but that girl must have been from an area with a different climate and better irrigation.

It'll be easier on the way back, without this thing in my arms, I console myself, and the way to the beach is shorter, it goes through olive groves, vineyards and scorched gardens, beside courtyards with barbed-wire fences where furious Alsatians and Dobermans hurl themselves against them, and through an underground tunnel in the stream, which acts as a passage-way for school children.

We used to drag ourselves through there once when we were attacking the Iroquois Brothers or drawing up a truce with them on no-man's land.

Parents used to put ordinary wooden ladders on either side of the road so that their children didn't have to run across the highway. In summer, the tunnel was dry and full of green lizards. Problems arose when the streams swelled, and the impatient kamikaze outlanders, accustomed to living with the road, threw themselves in front of herds of metal buffalo.

Every kilometre along the highway, there is a bouquet of plastic flowers in a plastic vase and a wooden cross, lamps, candles, even real marble tombstones with the faithfully engraved smiling faces of the deceased. a whole small town has bled to death on the road here. Every thirteen year-old has a scooter cobbled together from spare parts. a traffic accident in our country is death by natural causes.

'What're you thinking about?' I'll ask Ma as we leave the graveyard and go down onto the beach through the remains of an olive-grove above the old saltpans. The sun will have risen between the factory towers and the bell-tower and will be pouring burning honey over us.

'I'm thinking about conditioning, how we'll have to get conditioning, it's hotter every year. This could drive you mad.'

Sweat and dust will leave the imprint of muddy circles on her sandals and her heels, which she lifts in a sputtering rhythm. She has such small feet, a weak foundation for such heavy thighs; and a taut back and a face on which I recognize at most two express-ions, *talking head*.

31

'What about you?'

'I'm thinking I ought to fix up the scooter. I'll get it out of the shed for a start. I hope it still works, it's exhausting doing this walk every day. It's really too much.'

That's what we'll say to one another. And each of us will be thinking that today would be Daniel's birthday.

Daniel's death swallowed up the death of our young red-haired father, and all the previous deaths that had happened to us were caught up in it as well. Like a new love, I thought, new, and already ragged with all the earlier losses.

('Love and death are words without a diminutive,' said our neighbour the vet, Herr Professor. I tried: lovette, lovelet, loveling, deathlet, deathette, deathling... And augmentatives: death-and-a-half, super-death, super-love... 'Hey ho. There are no bigger or smaller words than them. Unlike life which is a lifelet,' sighed Herr Professor theatrically. He's that sort of guy, he doesn't really fit into the Old Settlement. He wore his hair combed back and he had a thin, sparse moustache on his fat face, above his full lips. He used to beam at us. He was different. He knew more than other people, he knew something about everything and expressed himself well, in a literary way. Apart from that, we found him somewhat nauseating.)

We laid the flowers down, a birthday gerbera-heart, on *our* grave, threw away the rotting plants, replaced the water. Ma swept the grave, while I sat on the edge beside the marble vase with Daniel's name, bored. Bored to death.

Ma and my sister watched a film recently where a woman goes mad after her child dies. So Ma said when she finally sat down beside me and lit a cigarette.

'And when after a while the pain eased, that woman, a fine lady, if mad, stopped a man in the street, a passer-by, and asked him whether she was alive.'

'Am I alive? she asked him,' Ma repeated vaguely, brushing bits of dry flowers from her dress.

'What happened to the woman afterwards?' I wanted to know.

'What d'you mean what happened?' said Ma. 'D'you know anyone who went un-mad?'

When we get back, outside the house, I see that all those winter shoes intended for cleaning have been left on the outside steps and now they're roasting in the sun. Among them are some men's boots, brogues and trainers, although the last time a man took his shoes off in this house was... four years ago?

Two pairs of shoes on each step, from the fifteenth to the third, as though some chance group of people who had found themselves in a column were coming down the steps. a funeral, a procession or wedding guests.

Daniel, my brother, died in his eighteenth year by jumping under a speeding Intercity Osijek–Zagreb–Split train. He threw himself onto the track from the concrete viaduct over the railway, one early winter morning. His body was found some twenty metres further on, in a vineyard.

'His blood was splattered everywhere, on the trees and the frozen leaves of the vines,' said people who, for the first few weeks, had made a pilgrimage to the site of the mishap; leaving, behind the St Andrew's cross, plastic roses and lamps that glimmered for as long as their batteries lasted.

Among my jottings, written on a notepad, I found this:

'Stay up, stay on the surface,' said my father, throwing me into the sea from the jetty. 'Swim, for god's sake, you've got long arms and legs,' he laughed out loud, with his tanned face and light eyebrows. And I swam, like a puppy, like every child.

Daniel jumped in after me and went under. Just a plop. Then nothing. That's the only time I ever heard Ma scream. She shrieked at my father. My sister shouted and wailed as

well, standing on the beach in her wet bathing suit, dropping
unchewed slimy pieces of bread and paté from her mouth. But
I could see that Daniel had stayed sitting on the bottom, he
wasn't even trying to come up.

'He's swallowed a bit of salt water,' my father repeated from
the sea, holding him.

Afterwards Daniel laughed and said: 'What's the big deal,
I was just teasing. Seeing who'd save me!'

They left me alone in the sea, for a moment, while they
brought him out.

'What're you thinking about now?'

'Cicadas. It's strange that we can't hear any cicadas. Had you noticed?'

It's as silent as a cave.

'It's really strange, maybe they've all burst.'

Everything is brightly lit, and yet I can't see anything. I cover my eyes with my hand and through the milky screen against that unbearable light I peer into the still olive-grove, full of evil silence and bad sun. I see my sun-tanned fingers and the thin white membrane between them. Behind them is the even sunnier beach, behind the beach is the empty prairie at scorching noon.

My hands will become even darker, my hair copper, my private places white in front of the mirror in my cold, darkened room.

But still, I never succeed in imagining the comfort of my room as I cross the prairie with a red-hot hat on my head, every time, every blinding Monday and Friday.

I try to step broadly and shallowly, to stay on the surface.

2

You didn't tell me how old you were?' he said.

'Seventeen,' I lied through my teeth and that made him smile.

He's quite a lot older than me. He has joined-together eyebrows above bright eyes.

'What're you doing at the market, this early?' he asked.

'Nothing much, looking at the fruit and vegetables, taking some photographs. Good colours.'

He had caught me off guard, in other words. In fact I was meant to be collecting news stories from the market about the vendors' strike; the camera was my room-mate's, a prop. An amazing new Konica-Minolta – with which neither fruit and veg, nor the old women at the market would need 'Photoshop' – they'd never have given me one like it at the office.

We had met three weeks earlier, he and I, at a party at *Shit.com* that was paying me to write or steal news for their site. I was good at re-working news from competitors' pages: copying, pasting and touching-up. Even its own author wouldn't recognize it. It was more than they deserved for the pittance they paid me.

The party was on the fifteenth floor of a skyscraper, and at that time I adored skyscrapers, lifts and all of that, life in the air, in the heights. Understandably, given that I had grown up, as it were in a depression, in a cleft between two houses.

I spent the whole evening being pestered by a scarecrow from Marketing.

Before she turned thirty she would 'sometimes knock back a little glass of brandy or dark ale,' she said, but that evening she was smashed.

'I'm totally smashed.'

Unusually, though, she told me the same three stories each time she met me in the corridor or when she found me sitting somewhere, drinking. The first story was about a colleague from the editorial office, who it was discovered, had once mistakenly phoned the mother of a colleague whom he fancied, moaning and saying: 'Oh, the things I'd do to you, *cara mia*.'

As it happened the mother was called Cara and she had a total fit.

'Too, too awful,' said my collocutor, opening her eyes wide and then bursting out laughing. 'But it's true,' she added, grabbing me by the elbow with her long nails, like a crab. The second story was about silicone implants and the possibility of breast-feeding when the woman had children, and the third about a Danish artist who was a cannibal.

She went from one person to another at the party, that crazy goose, repeating her stories, exactly the same each time. But people ignored her, turning back to those they were talking to, so she kept finding me and starting all over again. About the colleague who moaned into the telephone of someone's mother Cara, about implants and breast-feeding and about that performance artist in Copenhagen who ate fat from liposuction of the chin. In a moment of lucidity, she added delightedly that she had 'totally lost it, like a broken record' and went off to get some more wine.

That gave me time to escape. I wanted a refuge from this persecution, and I needed to lie down. My room-mate and the boy who drove us to the party had vanished without trace, into one of the bedrooms I assume, and I, dying of boredom, had to wait for a lift.

'I can't wait to be thirty,' my sister said before she became thirty. 'So that I can go home to bed at midnight, without being embarrassed.'

She used to say that often, I recall.

In the kitchen, people were throwing canapés with sea hare caviar at each other. In the room showing projections of old Disney cartoons, there were some partially dressed damsels lying around, while the guy with glasses showing the films rolled a cigarette and absently stroked the nylon-clad leg of one of the girls.

It was still too early for anything more daring so he put on some silent films. Who on earth would think of showing old films at a party, I thought. Perhaps they were the same people who listened to jazz at a wedding, and then everyone would go into an empty swimming pool and take each other's photos, turning it into a happening.

In the empty dining room, three guys on Ecstasy were singing a medley of Dalmatian songs, their arms round each other.

'Someone should exterminate them,' said the man with joined-up eyebrows and the pale eyes of a dingo. He appeared beside me in the doorway and smiled. He looked more sober than anyone else.

In the hall I noticed my persecutor staggering purposefully in search of a victim.

'Please,' I said to the dingo with joined-up eyebrows, 'if you've got a car, get me out of here.'

'You're white as a sheet,' he said, wrapping his jacket round me and leading me out into the wet street, where lights were playfully flickering.

'Have you had a lot to drink?' he asked me later, as he unlocked the door of his flat that smelled of newness, of polished parquet and Ikea furniture.

'Not really. Time of the month,' I explained like an advert for sanitary towels. 'That's why I'm not feeling great.'

'Ah,' he said. And pointed me to the toilet. 'Freshen up,' he said.

I stayed for a while in the black and white cloakroom, looking at the little women's bottles on the shelf. I touched each of them. I had never been with someone else's man before.

When I came into the room he was lying on his stomach without a stitch on, snoring. I took off my panties and lay down, naked, on his back, but he didn't stir. Towards dawn, when I was already asleep, he turned me over like a huge doll and parted my legs. I didn't manage to protest or draw him to me before we had both cried out. He once, at length. Me twice, but briefly.

The bedclothes were ruined, spattered with blood and semen.

'Look what we've done,' I said in the morning.

'What a pair we are,' he whispered into my hair, pulling me onto his chest, winding his arms and legs round me as though he had at least twice as many, like a hairy octopus. Maybe a spider, I thought.

Days later we ran into each other at the market.

'You didn't call me. And you said you would,' he said, hopping between the little mounds of Macedonian paprika and Golden Delicious apples. It was winter, freezing, white, noisy mornings and steamy evenings, full of smoke.

'Wait while I take your photo,' I said.

He posed with a stupid smile, paralysed with cold. Those eyebrows on his face looked like one big one. Later I lost that photo, or I left it in my flat, when I set off for home, to the Old Settlement, with no clear plan, apart from leaving Zagreb and not coming back.

'The last time was bloody,' I said as I pointed the lens towards him. 'I wasn't sure that you wanted to be reminded.'

'You really could be seventeen,' he said.

'Well, I am, in a way,' I said.

He took me home, we put the camera down on the little Ikea table, undressed and stayed together for two years.

Just before the end it sometimes happened that I shaved my armpits with his lady's razor and used her brush to do my hair.

With time everything becomes practical. Besides, it would be strange for me to be physically repelled by a woman whose husband I was sleeping with.

We produced the ineradicable strong, bitter smell of fresh milk.

Sometimes I wondered whether she could sense my presence in her apartment – saliva on the pillow, skin and hairs in the dust under the bed – or maybe he did a thorough job of clearing it all up.

What kind of... relationship was it? As soon as I approached, he would shove himself into me. Lying, sitting, standing, kneeling, he'd throw me onto my elbows, lift me onto the wall, a table, a tree, filling me.

I grabbed him. Kissed. Scratched. Hit. Gripped him, gripped him.

Stroked him, stroked him.

As we fucked, my arms grew out towards him, even face down.

On the morning my sister phoned about Ma, I was sitting naked in his kitchen, watching CDs, which were strung up on the balconies of the neighbouring building to scare the crows and pigeons, dancing in the wind. If I closed my eyes and ears tight, I could hear music from all directions in my head.

He had slipped out to the shop for some breakfast, he looked happy when I saw him for the last time, smiling with his dingo eyes. But by then I didn't love him any more.

I dressed unhurriedly and slammed the door shut.

The next day I left Zagreb and went to the Old Settlement.

It was forty degrees outside, in the bus probably only five, bitterly cold. The driver had put on the air-conditioning.

A short-legged white terrier crossed the empty road, so I couldn't even say that there wasn't so much as a dog in the streets.

'Rusty,' said a female voice, grabbing me by the shoulder.

I was sitting with my forehead stuck to the dirty window of the bus that went from the bus-station, through the car-ferry port into the outlying housing developments. I had shoved my suitcase behind my feet. Houses, mostly without facings, but some white, various colours, were rising up in Tetris hills and hillocks at great speed. Every time I raised my head, on the hill in front of me there were yet more unfinished cubes with satellite antennae. The wind blew the soil off those hills, while goats had long ago devoured the original vegetation. In summer the north wind brought fires, and above the houses, on the mountain, black pines grew. Here and there one caught sight of a bush of Maquis, prickly broom or a palm with tiny inedible dates.

I stared at the face of the woman who had roused me from unconsciousness. The bus had left the bus station and the doors hissed shut.

'Rusty, I hasn't seen you in an age... why've you come? Eh?'

Her skirt was tugged right up under her breasts; she was wearing shiny, lacquered pink boots with broken heels. She was swaying over my head, holding onto the strap with one hand.

Only someone from the Old Settlement could have called me Rusty.

'You've forgot me...'

Inflamed eyes under a shock of bleached, almost white curls.

'You've forgot me. Maria Čarija. The Iroquois' cousin, for God's sake!'

To the delight of the passengers, she tapped her open mouth with outstretched fingers briefly and jerkily several times, producing the old war cry of her tribe from the railway track by way of greeting.

She laughed with large yellow teeth, a young woman. What was with her hair? It stuck up in places in long and short thick white tufts, and in places there was none at all. Maria Čarija. That face.

'Why've you come? Why've you come?' she asked through her cracked lips.

'I remembers you,' I said quickly. 'I've come. The world goes round, and you always comes back to the same place.'

'You's never does remember me,' she said loudly, right into my face.

Now the other passengers were looking at us quite openly, but cautiously, as you look at a spectacle involving two lunatics. If only I wasn't dressed like this, in red. If only I wasn't so tall. If I were smaller, paler, more functional.

'But I knows you. Oh yes, I knows you.'

She laughed with her big yellow teeth, hopping from foot to foot. She had followed Daniel secretly, couldn't stop pursuing him, there was nothing to be done – he was like a magnet to her.

I push my case towards the door. There are still four stops before mine, I hope I'll be able to walk that far. She had come close to my cheek. I noticed the locks of her hair had been pulled out, drawing blood.

'I knows your brother too. I knows who killed him,' she whispered.

'Oh, of course you do, why don't you tell it all,' I muttered crossly, to myself.

The harmonica-like middle of the bus shifted under my feet. The doors hissed again and in the next shot I saw from the pavement

Čarija's face pressed against the bus window. She was licking the glass and smiling, cheerily, without malice.

And so I had made it. Yes, I'd made it! I'd returned to my hometown: nothing more than a vast rubbish dump, mud and olive groves, glorious dust, evenings on the empty terrace of the Illyria hotel, heavy metals in the air, excrement and pine-woods, cats and slippery fish scales on the greasy slipway and the sea stretched out as far as November, when the north wind gets up.

On my route home, I see shopping malls and forests of jumbo posters, tundra and sorrowful bungalows on the road, but before that I pass along brightly-lit walkways. Down below are the cruisers in the passenger harbour, guides with their arms in the air in front of a column of Japanese and American pensioners with prostheses and toupés; casinos, the mild winds of hashish, the stench of bodies and perfume; acid, trans-folk as well as Saint Tropez, Monte Carlo, Cista Provo, *belle dame sans merci*, girls in high heels squeezed into white nylon and animal skins; clean-shaven lads jingling the keys of polished cars, their hands, as they touch my face, smell of vinyl and genitalia, money and tobacco.

Music blares, handfuls of worthless coins are scattered over the copper bar top. *Salon Sodom. Cafe Eldorado.*

There, on the glass and granite quay, while the yachts sail out of the harbour, the workers who swear that they destroyed communism are on strike. Their thinning hair is tied in ponytails, some have bad teeth, all have large hands and look younger than their wives. They sit around the fountain, among the trampled begonias, Indian figs and dog mess, smoking *York* or *Marlboro* and saying that nothing's going to change that'll do them any good.

In the early hours, after midnight, women and men take off their clothes, discard their sandals and go into the sea. They stand and immerse themselves in the sandy shallows. Girls and young men drink long cocktails out of thin glasses. Some foreign students lie on their backs, their legs together and wave their arms to leave the imprints of wings. That game in the sand is called drawing angels.

The summer night has replaced the day in the flaming centre of the town, under the moon's bloody wink.

That is where I shall erupt from the total darkness of a side street and pass through a scene like this, pure and flat as a drawing – and come out of it appalled that so much life goes on without me.

My suitcase clatters along behind me, a faithful wheeled dog. Even if someone had picked me up and shaken me upside down, I wouldn't have had enough cash for a taxi. People pass me in noisy groups: They are showered, with loud waves of brilliantine in their hair, while I smell of sweat and the sour bus. My short dress sticks to my back and legs.

I look round several times, afraid that Čarija will appear behind me and spit into my hair. We used to do that at one time. I'm almost ready to give the daft bitch a hiding, because of today, because of every yesterday and day before yesterday, because of things that aren't connected and because once, long ago her brothers cut my head open with a stone.

Maria had always been in the background: a silent Iroquois from that bellicose tribe. If she so much as made a sound, one of her relatives would bash her with a stick or turn on her with a 'None of your crap'. Later her status improved – when it transpired that not one of the Iroquois, not even Tomi, could fire an air gun as accurately. When the fair came to town at New Year, the Iroquois Brothers took her to the shooting gallery and afterwards exchanged their trophies – lucky charms and teddy bears – with the gallery manager for a bottle of Ballantine's.

'Iroquois Maria can hit a bird's eye in flight,' the lads said.

But I remember her most clearly in connection with our ginger Jill.

It was Daniel who brought us ginger Jill. When he was little, we often lost him in the labyrinth of streets. He would wander

Daniel, the strutting warrior, handsomer than anything you could find in the streets of the Settlement, helped him, soothing the brindled kitten with his dirty hands.

For my brother Daniel, who had just discovered video games, the cat was a space oddity, a furry projectile and little galactic trooper.

But my father, as soon as he saw her, said: 'Well, just look at her, the little star, what a coat, what bearing, à la Claudia Cardinale!'

So she became Jill, as in *Jill McBain* from the Sergio Leone film, 'Once Upon a Time in the West'. We wanted to please our father.

Not long after, the Iroquois Brothers came into our street with their heavily armed, little half-witted Maria, to fetch their cat Mikan. My father easily persuaded them that Jill – was Jill that she couldn't be Mikan, that she didn't have balls, that she had fallen out of the sky, what else.

Later, nevertheless, that stone was hurled at my head – from the back I looked very like my brother.

My father bequeathed to his sorrowful *amigo* his leather belt, the parrot and an old silver Colt – he had bought it specially for him, for his birthday, and it 'had once been able to fire real bullets', Daniel said. He roamed through the streets of the settlement, got up like that, even after he emerged from his childhood years. He always walked in a diagonal, in an unpredictable tacking movement, trying to trick the murderer *Liberty Valance* or the greedy *Pacman*. Or to capture the cyber badge of the universe, like a cyber cowboy.

And the rest of us walked like that too, tacking, the aim of the game being to obstruct an invisible enemy sniper. There weren't any snipers in the Settlement, but just in case.

The parrot didn't interest Daniel much. She strolled along the top of the dresser, cackling. She was waiting for her master, our father, and then she forgot who or what she was waiting for, but she still went on standing up there, waiting.

Ginger Jill spent a long time stalking the crazy bird, lying in wait for it, the little hyena.

off or disappear from a game without saying a word. But the Old Settlement had natural boundaries, like every peninsula, and there wasn't anywhere to go. Sea on three sides, on the other desert: the railway, brambles, and along the shore, dust. Now there's a fresh grass carpet like a golf course and the glazed cubes of shopping malls.

That time we found Daniel on the slipway, as usual, behind a crane and the boats in dry dock, playing with young Jill. She was blind in one eye, covered in fleas and she stank of wood preservative. The slipway always reeked of the rotten undersides of sick boats, between whose wooden ribs oil glistened in the stagnant sea-water. Decay was the smell of my childhood, not even the sun managed to do much about that.

He tried to persuade us that ginger Jill had dropped out of the sky. There was no other explanation, Daniel insisted, because there weren't any trees or buildings above the slipway from whose roofs she could have fallen onto the tarpaulin and fish crates, there was only the sky.

'She fell out of the sky,' he said. He had already entirely convinced himself of this story, so there was no point in getting cross with him.

Later it turned out that he had taken the kitten from the outlanders, that it was Maria's favourite.

Maria spent the whole day miaowing, running across the field calling the kitten, we discovered.

But by that time we had already taken the little animal to the ve

Herr Professor examined the creature, rubbed an ampoule anti-parasite stuff into the fur on her back and explained som thing to Daniel with undisguised adoration.

Daniel turned up the sleeve of his pullover and scratched a sc on his elbow. There was something coquettish about him, now t I think about it, even when he was biting his nails or squatting the toilet. And, like all genuine coquettes, he appeared enti unaware of it.

'Dirty great paedophile,' my sister whispered of our neighl as we stood at the door of his kitchen in which there was n any heat, even in winter.

In the end all that was left of the parrot's puffed-up pride were a few bloody feathers on the tiles and her untouched beak.

That all happened not long after Daniel's funeral. No one was thinking about the unfortunate bird, which ought to have been shut up in a cage, out of reach, I recall.

Later, my sister cleared up the mess, and turned with a broom, full of righteous anger, on ginger Jill who was calmly licking herself with her pink tongue. Jill is a wily and elastic little beast and my sister assumed she had made herself scarce until the dust settled.

Later we went to look for her at our neighbour's. She was lying on the floor tiles cleaning her tail just as she had been when we last saw her.

We adored ginger Jill, full of electric indifference under our stroking palms. It was easy to construe indifference as wisdom.

'Bloodthirsty sphinx,' said Herr Professor, as soon as she had grown into a huntress.

Had ginger Jill been the size of a dog, I thought, she would have slit my throat as well. Sooner or later all cat owners come to believe that. But as it was, she had to accept my love and concern.

And like all cats with a modicum of self-respect, it seemed as though she was on the point of speaking and so we deliberately attributed several powers or inexplicable events to her.

I know something about cats, but neither the Cheshire Cat, nor Snowball, nor Simone Simon nor Natasja Kinski, nor the fiery Behemot, nor Louis Wain's cat, not one of them had that elegance, that self-sufficiency and commitment of an actress in love, of which no one could ever be sure whether they were just putting it on. Probably, but that didn't matter too much to the actors.

'Jill is devil-ificent,' said Daniel, looking at her.

'Why aren't I a cat? That's my real nature,' said my sister, watching Jill stretch.

And Jill was our household devil-ificence, but nevertheless, we would have coldly skinned her alive because of our father's parrot had we caught her in the act.

I sat beside the fridge on the tiles with the dirty black grouting, absentmindedly peeling off a Fanta sticker, while my sister cleaned the bloody marks from the floor with *Vim* and a scrubbing brush, from time to time emitting shrieks of revulsion and fury, shooting a glance at me as though I was the one who had slit the bird's throat.

Where had he been hiding all these years, that old guy we called Herr Professor, I wondered as I ambled towards the Settlement, through this town that never sleeps in summer. He must have gone a really long way away. He left without a word and all that reached us from him was a telegram of condolence, stunned, I'd say – three whole weeks after Daniel's death. There was also a short letter, with no sender's address, which we presume came from him. The letter was addressed to Daniel, and it arrived a week too late for him to have received and read it. It was postmarked Perm and the stamp had a picture of Laika the Astrobitch on it.

July was on the wane, the night heat was bursting out of the ground, in protuberances of earth, bumps in the asphalt – there had been no rain for more than two months. I was still several kilometres from the house and it was several hours before morning. Behind me was Zagreb, distant, more distant than Perm, than Osaka and Juneau, and Santa Fe, the most distant city on earth.

'That's what the towns where you abandon your failed illusions are like,' our favourite cowboy Ned Montgomery would say, riding off into the sunset with a cigarette between his teeth.

After a while, in the Old Settlement, we began to avoid Herr Professor. Stories were going around. People stick a stinking badge on you, which everyone can see apart from those who have been marked like that – they even wonder where the stench, *wtf*, is coming from. Like when you tread in dog dirt, and don't realize that what's smelling is *your* shoe.

Even Jill, with instinctive feline opportunism, avoided our neighbour's doorway, even though she would have found bits of skin and meat in the kitchen, and mice and lizards in the garden.

Daniel, who lacked any curiosity about village intrigue and scandal mongering – but who was passionately and joyfully curious about animals – used at one stage to go on whole-day visits to the vet's. But with time, he too stopped going, I recall. That was shortly before the *incident*.

At the time the *incident* occurred, I was thoroughly settled in Zagreb, so that I can't say all that much about it. My brother had just begun to hang around with Iroquois Tomi, the younger Barić and some of his other local contemporaries, my sister told me. They mended motorbikes and got up to the usual secondary-schoolboy foolish things. '

Later word went round that Tomi and Daniel and some of the other Iroquois Brothers had thrown stones at a bus on the route Old Settlement – Northern Habour – Centre and almost killed the driver. But that wasn't true, Ma said.

It seems that this was the work of Ear and Tiny, my sister affirmed. I knew Ear and Tiny, two jerks who dressed like Puff Daddy and Eminem.

Now all the actors in that story are corpses.

Ear was sent to a San Patrignano home and all trace of him was then lost. Some say that his body was found burned in a container, somewhere near Ancona.

Tiny had a whole barrel-full of bullets emptied into him by a stranger, from behind, as he rode his Vespa.

The younger Barić was killed on the road. He was walking along the tarmac and taken out by a drunken truck-driver. I'm really sorry about him, he wasn't crazy.

When the *incident* occurred, when Herr Professor was beaten up and his apartment trashed, I recall, all those lads from the Settlement were summoned to the Police Station. Including Daniel.

Ma was beside herself, my sister said.

'The man was almost done for,' said Ma, meaning Herr Professor.

'Dear God, I'd prefer he was killed himself rather than have him kill anyone else,' said Ma, meaning my brother.

It ended with the vet making a statement that it was not those lads, Daniel's pals, the papers reported.

Soon afterwards, Herr Professor left the Settlement, while 'the perpetrators were not found', it was reported, I recall.

People carried on gossiping. That the vet had got a job with the UN Peacekeeping force, looking after the army dogs, that he had worked his way through half the soldiers or they through him – stories like that were extremely popular at the time – and had finally moved to the Netherlands with a young UN employee.

It was also said that he had a clinic on the other side of town, also that he had married a woman vet with whom he was living in a basement with a little garden, but there were no children.

Ma was convinced that she had seen him once at the Bazaar, stealing a walnut from a pile on a stall, he had passed on quickly, presumably afraid of the stallholder and Ma would have called to him to say hello, but she simply couldn't remember his real name.

And now he's come back.

'That old gay's back,' said my sister when she called me in Zagreb, after she had opened the conversation with a desperate: 'I don't know what to do with her.' Meaning Ma.

'I can't leave her like this, but I have to go back to work, I've got revision for those losers with re-sits.'

Then a sigh.

Then: 'Hell.' And: 'You thinking of coming?'

'Not that soon,' I said, the day before yesterday in Zagreb.

And then my sister said that, that the man I'd given up looking for had come back.

As though I'd been summoned from a stuffy waiting room after I'd already given up the ghost five or six times, I thought.

It took me half an hour to pack a bag with everything I could cram into the idea of my life.

'The number you have dialled is currently unavailable,' maintained the answer-phone on my sister's mobile when I got off the bus and called her. It was already late, I observed, they would be asleep.

Ginger Jill slept on Mother's feet, Ma lay on her back like a corpse, with a burnt-out cigarette in her fingers, while my sister up in the attic slept with her hair in a firm night-time plait, curled up, with a pillow over her head. *On way home. Be there early morning.* Press. *Sent.*

𝓬

Make something of your life, they say. But what can you make of your life if you don't have money for a taxi? Your old man never set foot in a taxi. Your old lady never set foot in a taxi. And you live in a country where such a thing is expensive, a privilege. I can see you'll never marry. No-no-no, don't get annoyed. You're not bad, and you've got a nice jacket, but you're a one-off. Try to make something of your life, get an education, if you've got connections, let them sort you something where you won't slave for peanuts, but know this – if your old man never set foot in a taxi, there's only the remotest chance that you will and that's the way things are. a brave insight into that fact is the most you'll achieve in life. Such are the times, such is the place. You and I will always have enough for a decent pair of shoes, because we know that decent shoes are the most we can have. You and I will always have decent shoes: we need them because we don't have money for a taxi.'

That's what the guy at the bar said. He sat down beside me, slurping his beer.

Tubby Diana had turned off the music after the police intervened.

In front of the building, by a parked BMW, some lads had got together over a bottle of Chivas Regal. You could hear the kitsch blaring even through the closed doors of the car.

Diana was drying glasses. She had *that* expression on her face, like abused women who have given up on themselves. But still on a knife-edge.

49

'If you said *boo*, she'd have a heart attack,' said my sister. But that's the same expression women here have if they don't have a man and they're past twenty-something. Hey-ho. Where did I go wrong? The girls who never left the Old Settlement didn't have a lot of choice.

Some became surfers' babes, others motorcycle molls.

'Born groupies,' said my sister.

'Born to be wives,' she said.

Diana herself had married a boy from the Settlement for whom his Yamaha was the be-all and end-all. He shortened the exhaust and sped past her house until she married him, I recalled.

'Rats,' yawned the guy at the bar, glancing through the door at the lads by the BMW.

'Oh, leave them be,' Diana smiled bleakly. She wanted to go home without gunshots and sweeping up glass. Me too, I thought.

'Racketeers,' muttered the guy in our direction. One of them seemed familiar to me, as though I'd seen him at one time in Daniel's company, when I used to come home from uni. But when our eyes met, he turned his head away, quickly.

I've known Diana my whole life. We all called her Tubby Diana, because she had been a tubby child. Now she's thin, but the Tubby has stuck. She's no older than me, and she has two little sons with the biker, twins, and her face is puffy.

'All the local lasses are bloated with alcohol by their twenties,' said the guy, tipsily. 'Maybe that's your fate as well. Accumulating fluid,' he informed me.

Diana could give me a lift home when her shift ends, I'd thought, as I dragged my suitcase along and caught sight from the street of the familiar pink neon sign of the *Last Chance* with its painted green palm.

'Sure, old thing,' she had said, 'no problem.'

It was almost day.

There weren't many customers at the *Last Chance*, closing time was in the air.

The fellow at the bar, an old guy sleeping with his head on the table ('Dipso' said the g.a.t.b.), four Swedish tourists at the separate table ('swingers', said the g.a.t.b. between two gulps), and right at the back, beside the door to the toilet, a mysterious good-looker playing a mouth-organ.

Well, well, I thought. What film was this?

A foot on the edge of the table and a blue tuxedo. He was leaning his head and shoulders against the wall. Playing.

Foreigner, I thought.

'Phoney?' I asked the guy at the bar, rolling my eyes in the direction of the lad in the gloom.

'Nah! That's Angelo!' said the guy.

'Hey, Tubby, take Angelo a Southern and give the kid a cognac! And another big one for me!' he rolled the empty beer bottle across the bar.

Diana looked at him grudgingly. The guy owed her.

'To hell with that!' the guy pulled a face. 'Write it down. Just write it down, I say.'

The good-looker in the corner blew twice into his harmonica to clear the dust, then launched into a familiar tune. *Yippee ya yo. Yippee ya yay.*

3

The kid did a thorough job. He wanted to be sure he wouldn't survive,' the inspector had commented.

They found Daniel's body immediately, some twenty metres from the viaduct, in a vineyard, and his left arm only two days later, in a stream under a spruce bush.

'You're lucky, the part that was in the water wasn't got by vermin,' said the coroner when we had made our way down the long staircase into the hospital's basement mortuary. They had somehow attached the arm for the identification.

Blood had spurted all over the place, over the trees and the frozen vine leaves, said people who had made a pilgrimage to the place of the mishap for the first few weeks, leaving plastic roses and lamps that lasted as long as their batteries did behind the St Andrew's cross.

'A performance,' my sister had said as we approached the railway line.

On the day of the funeral some relations whom I barely knew drove me from Zagreb.

They crammed six adults into the car, it was drizzling and we were all given a salami sandwich for the journey. The air was sour as were the salami and the drizzle.

Later, in the evening, as my sister and I drew near to the railway, I was still feeling sick from that air in my nostrils. My sister wanted to get it over quickly, and dragged me by my moist, limp hand, as though we were children, she held it for a while in her own cold, dry one, digging her little sharp nails into my palm.

In the mortuary, I looked at my brother's right hand, on which the nails he'd always bitten down to the quick had grown in the meantime. Because of those nails that had grown I would've known he was dead, even in my sleep.

'It's Daniel,' I said, although the puppet with the small head lying on the metal table no longer had anything to do with him.

He didn't leave any kind of letter.

'They don't usually leave any, actually,' people told me.

'Get over it, doesn't everyone leave without a message, what's so strange?' said my sister.

What do I know about *everyone*, I thought. It wasn't like Daniel, I thought, to go without a word.

Some people I half knew wept without ceasing and that drove me out of the house. I remember that one lady in black, who used to frequent funerals, sat in the hall, in the corner under Mother's old hair dryer, sobbing and blowing her nose noisily, so that she looked like a desperately grieving woman at a hairdresser's.

'Masochists,' said my sister. 'They didn't even know him. Perverse.'

Once, as children, we'd been at a funeral in the hills, where a professional mourner had been brought in, paid to wail and so inspire other people to cry. I think she was exceptionally successful as I too began to cry, from pure horror. Then my sister said: 'They've terrified the kid, masochists.'

That was the first time I heard that word.

The years – from the day when the police rang the bell, and Ma opened the door – passed in a flash, but I remember that unknown lady in black under the hair dryer better than any of the three of us.

Between my brother's death and my sister's almost incidental phone call that brought me back home, nothing worthy of mention happened, at least not to me.

I returned to the Old Settlement, for the answer to my question, for the words that my brother had sent to some fourth person, not to my mother, nor my sister, nor me. That's what drives me to keep walking, turning over every stone. And, if truth be told, all I've discovered in my roaming and turning over, is that the world contains more stones than snakes and bugs under them.

'Yawn and stretch as much as you can,' ginger Jill told me in an ancient dream. And I obey her, because every cat that speaks, even in a dream, deserves attention. I am waiting on a bench in the deep shade of a carob tree for my host to appear, I yawn and stretch in the scorching, endless, hypnotic Settlement afternoon. Lethargy, they call it, when a place hypnotizes you.

In the silence, from the other side of the garden, over the wall, purple figs can be heard thudding onto the ground, their tree, abandoned to itself, having gone wild like the beanstalk up which that idiot wanted to climb to the sky.

Through the brightly coloured strips of plastic of the curtain in the doorway, Herr Professor appears and places a tray of cold tea and cakes on the garden table.

'*Petits-fours*', he says.

He stretches out his fleshy legs with their strong white calves and from time to time rubs one pink heel against the other. On the other side of the courtyard, beside the broken greenhouse, with two stunted lemon trees, their branches pruned, a pair of tortoises are mating. 'They're a bit late this year,' says the Professor. The female doesn't stir, while the male has opened his little mouth wide. There are a few stiff, dirty rags on the washing line, with flies and flying ants landing on them, and from the garden, tap water drips persistently into the yellowing stone basin.

I bend towards the iced cakes, but the Professor stops me with a movement of his hand. Something is noiselessly rolling towards us.

'Listen!'

Cymbals clang and stop the air.

'It's St Fjoko's Day,' Ma had concluded this morning at breakfast.

'St Fjoko,' I say out loud, reaching for a cake.

'Aha, the town saint's day!' The Professor slaps his thighs.

'Vrdovđek just bought it. The brass band.'

'Vrdovđek, oh yes. The one with all the shops?'

'Shops, and everything in the Settlement. He's the big shot now,' I say.

I watch the Professor: his face, his blinking eyes, large hands, so white they're almost blue. Over the years, his physical resemblance to a drowned man has become more obvious. And with those whiskers and that moustache – like a catfish, really. Whales and dolphins returned to the sea, disappointed with life on land, but the Professor's type of sea creature had remained forever in between, wedged. He had once kept salamanders in formalin in glass jars in his living room, the way people in the Old Settlement keep pictures of their closest relatives. He also had two salamanders ('two fiery dragons', he said), but I think all those jars were shattered in the *incident*.

With a rolled newspaper, he attempts to drive away the flies attracted by the cakes. As he swats them, scampering round the table, he is no less formal and pompous than he was a little earlier with the tray, I observe.

'He's got manners, that man,' Ma once said. She always overrated politeness.

'His whole family, especially his late mother, was very refined. Crème de la crème,' said Mother's relative Mariana Mateljan. And added: 'God knows who this waster takes after.'

He kills several horseflies and smaller flies and sits down right beside me. He smiles like a pile of gelatine, slightly triumphantly and 'in that name' opens a special cutglass bottle. The liquid in the bottom of the glass looks like the fluid in which the amphibians on the vet's sideboard had once swum. I can't avoid that image, although I recognize the smell of rose liqueur, honey-sweet and sharp.

'Rose liqueur,' *the insatiable one* used to say. 'Oops-a-daisy! That'll warm those fine ladies up. Give 'em a couple of glasses, they all starts cooling themselves with their skirts. They hauls their dresses up over their knees and airs themselves. The whole street'll stink of cunt...'

'The larger the cymbal, the deeper the sound and the longer it lasts, it behaves like spilled mercury,' says Herr Professor, handing me a silver teaspoon.

The light here is very soft and perhaps that, combined with the brass band and the liqueur, is why I am feeling lethargic.

Now that I was finally within reach of him, I had kept putting off the meeting like an exam or a visit to the doctor, but in the neglected garden belonging to that gelatine gentleman whom I do not wish to touch with even a millimetre of skin or clothing and of whose breathing beside me I am all too conscious – I feel that, after so many years of dragging my heels, I have sat down beside water, to rest. I have arrived somewhere. If nothing else, I am no longer being tormented by the need to get up and walk.

The timpani announce summer; the brass band declares the beginning of a cheerful holiday, even if it only lasts a few moments.

'Even a bear can play the cymbals,' my sister said on one occasion.

But I like cymbals. Without them a marching band would be less exciting.

'Cymbals and trumpet, that is, dear Dada, true theatre! In the street! In our Long Street!' Herr Professor beams, like a returned exile.

He had polished the brass plate on his flaking front door, I observed: *Small Animal Veterinary Clinic. K. Šain.*

'Karlo Šain, good name for an opera conductor or someone's uncle,' said my sister, long ago.

'Your buddy's a faggot, you clown,' she said, slapping Daniel's bum when he began visiting the vet frequently, as though he had bird flu.

'Fag, fag,' she taunted, making that shameful gesture with her hand and fist. Daniel would respond with another gesture, careless, twisting his finger against his temple, I recall.

Although she was never what you might call a beauty, my sister could, even then, have had a lot of men – for her sake one had already dived off the Big Pier onto the rocks, but he didn't make it to the sea, or her attention. Tenderness in her had solidified like sugar on which you break your teeth. My sister always expresses caution as far as love is concerned, I observed. That stiffness doesn't fit with her lips like a wound or her smooth dark skin. 'Camouflaged,' Daniel called her if she wasn't in the room with us.

Whoever met my brother wanted to take him home, to have him nearby laughing or speaking, to be Daniel, to touch him on the shoulder, to pinch his cheek (which he hated). He had the gentleness and ferocity of a serious little man. Well, tenderness attracts people in different ways, it tempts some to crush it, I recall, people often wanted to thrash him; it gets on some people's nerves. Being just a little bit different was always an excellent reason for something to be destroyed.

I see them: my older sister and my younger brother sitting arguing, their heads close together, so that Ma wouldn't hear them: side by side like that, they looked like a cactus and its flower.

Keeping company with the vet developed into friendship the autumn my brother started secondary school. That year Daniel made a terrarium in the Prof's garden: over dry sand that he had carried from the Little Lagoon. Glided lizards, transparent little tarantulas and a blasé *gecko*, a big greenhorn, a real dandy; he had fireflies and scarab beetles and two tortoises, you could tell the female by her cracked shell, I recall. They survived and are still here in the garden, beside the clouded glass of the greenhouse, which 'bore witness to the fact that this house had seen better days,' said my sister once. The Professor's yard, enclosed by a stone wall with little sparkling pieces of mother-of-pearl in it, the bodies of shell-fish, and its crawling, rattling, grunting animal kingdom, attracted us, all of us children, I recall. We used to go there almost stealthily, because of those stories. Apart from Daniel, who, by all accounts, had no problems of that kind.

Later I observed behaviour similar to ours in people who privately, to themselves, admire things that they will gladly vilify in public, equally sincerely and fervently. That must be painful, I thought. Depends on the person, I think now.

It seemed that everything was simpler for Daniel. He came here every day for as long as he felt like coming. Perhaps that's why my younger brother is more present in this yard than in our house.

It's still strange, I find myself thinking, that Daniel won't now appear through the colourful plastic strips in the Prof's doorway.

This is all that remains of his games, those two debauched tortoises, the already brittle posters for cowboy films that I had moved to my own room, and this Herr Professor here.

The only other possession of my brother's that I regretted was the Colt our father had given him, which we never found, along with his school case.

In my pocket I have a letter, which has been folded and unfolded countless times. On a dirty piece of paper, typed on an old type-writer, it says:

Dear Daniel,

I'm sorry I haven't written before now. The circumstances are such that I rarely open my electronic post, and I don't have access to a computer here. In fact, it's a lucky chance that I did read your messages at all. As you see (postmark), my work has taken me to the other side of the world. You're clever and you probably know that I'll need more time than has now passed to accept some of the things that happened, but I blame myself for this more than I do you. This stamp, of course, is not random, it's for you, as is the picture of the spotted salamander I'm sending you. I hope you'll like it. These are things I can't send by email, so I'm sending them by good old postal coach! There, let them be signs of reconciliation and good will. You write about the difficulties that have befallen you—I hope that you'll be able to solve those problems and that they aren't a consequence of that unpleasant event. I'd like to be able to help you. However, at present I can barely help myself, I sleep in some rather strange and miserable places, I eat when I manage it, that's how things are. It seems as though I've acquired pneumonia as well. For the moment I'm still not in a position to send you an address where you could write to me, or to promise that I'll be able to read your emails for the foreseeable future, but I hope it won't be long before I can. I'll let you know. Keep well.

Greetings,

Your Friend

In the upper right corner there is a date, several days after Daniel's death.

I wasn't impatient, and I wasn't rushing anywhere.

I had left several messages on his answerphone – I knew he was just a few metres away, the man who had the answer, behind the walls that divided his garden from the rest of the Settlement; and I believed that he would look for me. I turned several times into the short side street where his house was, but at the last minute my will failed me or I would be overcome by a comical and terrible shame or unease.

Today the telephone rang as Ma was making coffee for herself and her relative Mariana Mateljan. Cigarette smoke swirled down the corridor from the kitchen, water gurgled in the pot on the hot plate. They were both staring at a soap.

Šain Karlo here, please, I would like... to speak to Dada... So, at last, dear Dada!

'Mariana's my oldest friend,' Ma would mention from time to time. 'And my close relative,' she'd add.

Mariana had been coming from the city centre in an orange *Lada* for decades – on Sundays, sometimes also on Wednesdays.

Then one of the two of them would say something they shouldn't have and Mariana Mateljan would vanish without trace for a week, a month, and once even for two years. a black fart of smoke would puff out of the *Lada's* exhaust and she would drive off furiously like an orange out of hell. The last time that happened, we wrote her off forever, but then she did appear again just after Daniel's death.

I did not wish to disturb your dear mother... Otherwise, I would have got in touch myself, had I known that you... Had I known that you had come. Yes, yes, I did, I got your messages, but – I was away. Out of town on business. But, of course! It would be important for me, I would be glad if you came. Of cooourse... To remember the old days. Besides, besides...

'Hell, I thought we'd got rid of her, like the others,' said my sister when Mariana appeared among us again, with swollen eyes.

My sister polished her hatred of her to a high shine, I recall.

But still, Mariana finally found an appropriate role in our house and played it briskly and steadfastly. She was devoted to our ebbing Ma, Ma's misfortune brought Mariana freedom in their relationship. We knew – had it not been for Daniel's death, our relative would never have crossed the threshold of this house again.

Pride is such a bizarre attribute, and self-destructive; I'm not really clear why we count it a virtue.

For the first two weeks after Daniel's funeral, there would be up to thirty people in our house every day, they drank brandy, smoked and talked, and then suddenly, no one remembers the transition, they disappeared. Bit by bit, after some time, they stopped phoning as well. They probably didn't know what to talk about, it 'dis-com-mod-ed them all,' said my sister.

Mother sat and nodded the wax mask on her face up and down, like people on antipsychotic drugs when they come out of the madhouse, looking like robots or disinterred totems. My sister washed glasses ceaselessly, emptied ashtrays and sent piercing glances towards her soft, now former, husband. Tragedy swayed in the room, hanging from the ceiling light between the visitors and us.

'Someone else's tragedy, that requires commitment,' said my sister.

Come as soon as you can, come whenever you like. We're not far, we're neighbours, after all! Yes, yes, of course. Knock hard... my bell still doesn't work... on the door... 'Bye. 'Bye, my dear. '

I put the receiver down.

Mariana was sitting in a preparing-to-concentrate attitude in front of the television, cracking walnuts.

'It's our St Fjoko's Day today,' she said.

'He saved us from the plague,' she added, scratching her belly.

'And died of syphilis,' she said emphatically.

I guessed that this was the beginning of one of Mariana's bravura tirades, and they shouldn't be missed. I'll go this afternoon, *besides, besides.*

I've no clue what our Fjoko died of or why. His holy bone was carried up and down in a silver box behind the high cross along the one decent road in the Settlement. The Long Road leading from the port to the way out onto the highway.

On St Fjoko's Day, a band of male and female blowers, sweaty in their blue uniforms blares away all day, morning and afternoon. Towards evening the men from the brotherhood squeeze into cowls and set off in a procession with flaming torches, while behind them the nuns and women from the Church Choir of St Lisa sing monotonously.

Round the tail of the centipede that is twice as long as Long Road, the emotional populace mills with dignity. They mill, because Long Road is not particularly long and sometimes the procession's head catches up with its own tail.

'Dunque,' continues Mariana, licking honey from the piece of bread on which she has laid the walnuts, 'the future saint's embarrassing illness never stops him carrying on with his lovers. In fact, his body's falling apart, his bones is decaying, but his spirit's still lively. That's why merciful and almighty God left our martyr, for all he was syphilitic, untouched in the part that was for his devotees, as indeed for the whole town today, a holy relic – here, like this!'

She stretched out her fat middle finger with two gold rings and a long, polished nail.

'He never did!' I bleated. She sometimes imagined things, like every born storyteller who sacrifices truth on the altar of the story.

Everyone knows that Fjoko had a blessed finger whose touch cured lepers. So what was so fantastic about this, I asked her.

Mariana's body, covered in tinkling jewellery, in its wide tunic of dazzling brightness, had settled into the couch, but only in order to spread its crest.

'All depends,' she answered. 'Yous can lie to tell the truth. When all's said and done, in all the hullabaloo over St Fjoko there's a little bone from his middle finger, so you just have a think.'

She smacked her lips and lightly stroked her gold and silver rings over sleepy Jill who had snuggled in between the cushions.

Mariana has a long head, good-looking in a horsey way, and you can't say that horses aren't beautiful, but her body is enormous, it seethes even when it's still, creating ebbing and flowing tides around it as it moves.

Ma was smiling absently as she put out her cigarette. The ashtray was brimming with flat fag-ends and walnut shells. Then she immediately rolled and lit a new one and turned up the volume.

Aaron clasped Minerva in a passionate embrace.

Mariana wiped away an invisible tear with her thumb.

Beside her, Ma looked like a wax candle beside a lighted Chinese lantern, I observed.

Our relative waved her hands, pressing the heat and stench out of the room. She sank still more deeply into the couch, occupying all the comfort available. I thought about the way Mariana sucked in through her pores the comfort of whatever room she found herself in. Along with the comfort, all the kitchen smells and household dust and odour of Tiger Balm from Mother's skin entered into her as well. Created from all those particles, which she absorbed like a brightly coloured hole in space, her laughter swelled and bubbled out of the windows, while her imperial flesh gushed under her wide clothes.

'Some day she'll go into our kitchen,' my sister said once, and our kitchen is small, 'and she'll never be able to get out again.'

After the soap, we drank up our bitter Turkish coffee, listening to the clock ticking in the hall as in some distant period-pantry, muffled by many years of accumulated preserves that time had forgotten to abandon and move on.

Perhaps they were thinking about poor Aaron, a mulatto who dies of jealousy on a daily basis. The people, who occasionally pass under our windows, carrying benches and large pots for fish stew into Long Road, are surely thinking about the celebration, the feast day. I was thinking about the afternoon and about Herr Professor Karlo Šain, who still had to answer my question and whose neighbouring house suddenly seemed to me as though it were at the end of a forest.

That evening, beneath the window stood a young man with a mouth organ, only without the mouth organ – the good-looker I saw the night I arrived in town, at the Last Chance. I had already recognized him through the thin curtains by his silhouette. He was, evidently, waiting for someone on the corner behind the former Co-operative Building, directly opposite the baker's house. Like this, without his blue tuxedo, he looked like an ordinary lad, killing time.

Nevertheless, the boy is really nice-looking, I thought to myself. Handsome, they would say in books. One of those whom you could just look at for hours, and it would be interesting. Dark legs in white socks and grimy white trainers. Shoulders, bearing – is that indifference – eyes narrow between his lashes. He was kicking a squashed plastic bottle over the gravel, unaware of how striking he was.

'Angelo,' a tall passer-by in a hurry addressed him, that's how he had been greeted by someone in a Municipal Cleaning department uniform who had passed by a little while ago, pushing a cart with brushes and a black plastic bucket, that was the name that a thin little girl whispered to another, long-legged, laughing, as they glided past him on roller-blades.

After a while a woman came for him in a convertible, around thirty, dressed formally and elegantly: cream skirt, lilac blouse, fine and bright, and cream sandals with low heels. She was carrying a summer coat over her arm, under her armpits she had visible damp patches, her limbs were slender and firm, the tanned skin on them polished, shiny, her long hair gathered up into a bun.

'Like an advert,' Ma would say.

As he walked towards her little sports car, the young man looked up, towards the place where I was standing, leaning out. But I don't believe he saw me. The western sun was gleaming from the direction of the house.

Beside Angelo, on the sunny side, his short shadow glided, suddenly lengthening as he walked, reaching right up to the woman's feet, then touching them, covering them, stroking them.

Outside our building, the tepid, salt air was filled with motionless images without perspective. It was a world of theatre flats and vertical planes, which a cat can scuttle over or a child with a bloody knee pushing a scooter crosses in a few steps. This is the part of the day when birds go crazy above the factory chimneys, a ripe August afternoon in which the bare Settlement bakes under a heavy lid, and the sea evaporates.

'Sultry, heavy and desolate,' *the insatiable one* would say.

I had never considered burned-up landscapes ugly, only tedious; or desperate, if I was myself in despair. Not in a hundred years will this ever bloom into a paradise garden. No way, I thought.

The whole day the sky looked like an apocalyptic postcard.

'Divine Providence!' *the insatiable one* would observe of such dramatic stage designs. Because cumulus clouds had begun to gather in the west and the oppressive heat would be so intense that, although it was nearly evening, the wallpaper in the rooms would start to sweat, and the branches of the poisonous oleanders in the yard, scalded with damp, would droop to the ground.

People would walk with greasy, wet, faces and tap their barometers in disbelief when they predicted stormy weather and low blood pressure, sometimes unconsciousness. Inertia, in any case, and 'that's not laziness, but an acute sickness of the will,' my sister correctly observed.

The boy with the mouth organ and his escort (or, in fact, he's most probably the escort) had left the stage, so for a moment the street was empty and abandoned.

'Rusty's back!' shouted the little girl on the roller-blades to her friend, sailing into the frame. I waved to them. I picked up a hat and waved harder.

'Hey-ey, Rusty!' the little girls waved back.

On my way out I jumped over the shoes that Ma had forgotten and that were still baking on the steps; there was fresh seagull shit on some of them.

In Long Road, the suburb smelled of impending rain and incense from the impending procession, and some people were taking tables out for this evening's festivities. Like an apparition, down the street rode that old blacksmith on his horse, talking to someone on his mobile phone, hands free.

When the sun goes down I say: I'll go and look for a job, and then I wander. In fact, I wander from morning to night. On Monday and Friday mornings Ma and I follow the standard route from the graveyard to the beach.

'When I'm up there, I'm with them,' says Ma solemnly, in a high register like an amen.

'Go with her, she'll fall under a truck, she's so woozy in this sun,' my sister phoned to say.

So I accompany her. We're becoming like those mother/daughter pairs, which don't separate even when the little girl grows up. Only then it usually turns out that it's the daughter, rather than the mother, who's lost the plot.

Such pairs can often be seen in the more affluent districts, in better educated and well to-do families, also in families with no sons, I've observed. So we don't satisfy a single one of the criteria.

The mothers and daughters I'm talking about are often very similar physically and they dress in a similar way, but sometimes the mother is pretty and young, while the daughter is ugly or fat. They sit in the morning at Clio or Twingo and go to shopping centres and cafés together.

'Your younger sister?' passing acquaintances will enquire courteously.

And the mother and daughter smile equally courteously or the mad daughter will just keep going, while the mother feels uncomfortable and breaks off the chat.

The news here is that last Monday Super Mario clones came to our settlement, with little red caps and red boiler suits, and in a matter of days demolished and then began to rebuild the *Illyria*.

We passed the *Illyria* almost every day, so that we were able to follow that amazing development as on a speeded-up film. It was as though the cement contained some luxury substance that made the building rise like dough and be rejuvenated.

This reminded me of a programme about nature that Ma regularly watched – the credits would show a gaudy flower which germinated, swelled and burst into flower from an ordinary seed, in five seconds, and then, in the next five seconds in a new frame we would see an embryo becoming, in an incomprehensible transformation, a burly fellow, with the face of an urban peasant, but no doubt of a romantic disposition, because he picks the flower.

That sequence left me with a certain scepticism about the natural sluggishness of the eye.

A gust of wind briefly cooled the air, but it also washed all kinds of rubbish into the Little Lagoon – the main attraction being the corpse of a young shark – so on the whole I lounged in the shade with a towel spread out between fag-ends and peach stones, watching the boats moving round the little islands outside the bay, in the middle of the channel.

Mother would stretch out on the beach, picking from it a morning rosary of tiny shells and sea snails, smaller than a child's nail and delicately formed. She was more likely to be intrigued by a snowflake, filigree, or a word on a grain of rice than the Eiffel

Tower or the Sahara. She once bought special paints and drew miniature drawings on hollow eggshells. But that was before her narcotic phase, while she still had ambitions of a sort.

The sea in the bay is a dense colour and as stable as primeval soup. Later, around midday, little boys come and gambol extravagantly in the shallows, but first thing in the morning it is tranquil, apart from the sounds of building works from the direction of the *Illyria*.

I like the Little Lagoon more than the other beaches in the Settlement because of the five old pines whose crowns are so high that I have to turn my head upside down and gaze straight into the sky to see them, which makes me dizzy; and it's not exposed to the south wind, so that there has always been less tar than at the other bathing places, from which we returned with black marks on our pants, I recalled. The beach was edged with laurel and pittosporum, planted by a Czech doctor who had once lived above the Little Lagoon. Even today his house is still the nicest in the Old Settlement, 'far nicer than Karlo Šain's house,' said Ma. The pittosporum bushes were decorated with ice-cream wrappings and condoms, 'at least the Little Lagoon hasn't yet been totally shat to pieces,' said my sister.

On this little piece of the coast everything is in any case crumbling from disease, with the dignity of an aging alcoholic, who remembers more glorious summers, just as Mother remembers Split festivals with Vice Vukov and Claudia Villa.

Some ruins can definitely be beautiful even when they stink, but as far as the *Illyria* is concerned, it was always ugly, like all buildings built in the fifties.

'It was a lot uglier when it was new,' said Ma.

It didn't help that it was a hotel. I'd been inside it more than once and I'd not found anything that would justify the idea of a hotel: a pool with turquoise tiles or afternoon silence at Reception, even the towels weren't white and rough with a logo and the inscription HOTEL, but brightly coloured, ordinary, thin with washing. But still, the most important element was there: the smell of chlorine on the starched sheets, the smell of Indian tea and paté, the stench of other people's summer holidays.

People from the Settlement and tourists gathered outside the Illyria, every day, looking at the Super Mario clones and commenting.

'What's this?'

'What's this?'

'What-in-hell is this?'

'Vrdovđek has bought the *Illyria*.'

'Quesque c'est?'

'Che cosa è questo?'

'Das ist eine Baustelle.'

'Nein, das ist ein Freudenhaus!'

'C'est un hôtel.'

'Wrdovjack?! Was ist Wrdovjack?'

'Vítejte v mé zahrade!'

'Shtooo?!'

'Üdvözlöm! Üdvözlöm!' 'Delighted to meet you!'

Harum-farum-larum – hedervarum.

The very next day, someone had written, behind the Table of Lies, on the wall beside the former *Illyria*:

WOTS DIS DOIN ON OUR PATCH?

In our kitchen, Mariana Mateljan tells us that Ned Montgomery is coming to Croatia : it's in all the newspapers, and all the portals are also screaming. This is the second time, they report. The first time Ned was young and unknown in Yugoslavia and he died in one of the opening scenes of the film 'Winnetou', they report. Newer generations know him better as one of the first 3D heroes of computer games, they report.

That's a game with a lot of dead *cyber* cowboys in which the good guys, the player and Ned, if they're quick on the draw and have a bit of luck, win shiny Sheriff's stars. The aim is always the same: not to allow the son's of bitches to defeat you.

'Ned Montgomery isn't the kind of guy who bakes himself on a yacht on the Hvar waterfront, he doesn't sip cappuccinos on the Dubrovnik Stradun with bodyguards at his backside and he doesn't wave from a transparent capsule at us ordinary mortals, Balkanjeros, like other so-called stars,' said my sister, blessing the famous actor. Ned Montgomery is not overly talkative, in interviews he replies to questions: Yes. No. Naturally. Thanks.

He doesn't put on airs, they'd say in the Old Settlement.

Once a TV-journalist said: 'OK, Ned, I thought you were a bit of a lad.'

'?!'

'But how can you be a bit of a lad, if you've been with one and the same woman for twenty years now?'

'Well I'm a cowboy,' explained Montgomery, lighting a cigarette in the studio as though it was nothing to do with him.

'Somehow everyone realized that being a lad is bad news for a cowboy,' said Daniel.

That one and the same woman was the fabulous Chiara Buffa, an announcer and singer on Radio Italia, who later died tragically and to whom he had been introduced on a set by Sergio Leone, the newspapers wrote. There was once a whole supplement about them.

And Daniel said it didn't seem at all impossible that someone would be able to get it up for twenty years for Chiara Buffa.

Mariana Mateljan brought me the paper and showed me the article.

'Why look, dear God in 'eaven, that cowaboy from your room 'as come!' she said, shoving the paper under my nose.

The producer was the famous Ned Montgomery – it said in the *Spectacle* column. The popular actor and director of spaghetti Westerns, who embodied many of the legends of the Wild West – it said. Some scenes in the new film, which we discover is also some sort of western, will be shot on location in our neighbourhood.

Ned Montgomery, otherwise from these parts through his grandfather on his mother's side, had been a star as early as the nineteen-sixties and seventies, and his best known creations were in the films *Gold Dust, More Gold Dust in the Eyes, The Return of Virgil C.* and *Virgil C's Last Bullet*, blah, blah – wrote the journalist.

Daniel would've been delighted, I thought delightedly. This would've been news for him, even though years had passed.

'Good morning, cowboy!' my brother used to greet himself when he was in a particularly good mood.

'Good night, cowboys and Indians! Make it snappy,' our father would say, chivvying us to bed.

'I'm not a cowboy,' my sister would say.

'Nor an Indian.'

I moved the poster of Ned Montgomery into my room the day my sister and mother decided to rent out Daniel's room, with its own entrance, to workers and tourists. 'You can't just crumple up that cowboy with his six gold Colts and chuck him in the trash,' said my sister.

What had that legendary Ned from the poster been? Marksman, poker-player, lonely rider, Sheriff of Yumo district, protector of women, keen on kerchiefs and hats, a devoted and sincere friend of men and dogs, quick on the draw and dropping his drawers. He was kept company on one part of the wall by the true champions Eastwood, Wayne and Django.

I knew that Daniel would be ok with that.

The only role of Montgomery's that I remember well, really very well, is in *Virgil C's Last Bullet* when he's killed by Lee Van Cleef in the final showdown. It's unusual for the hero in a Western to die. That film was re-screened numerous times on Sundays at 5pm and we must have seen it every time. Virgil, the character played by Montgomery, had returned to his native Quentin, a small town he had abandoned in his eighteenth year, as I had mine, but on his return 'he had not found a single one of his tears,' whereas that was all I'd found in the Old Settlement.

One of the things I enjoy most as I roam through the streets is finding old graffiti on top of and underneath the peeling rind of façades.

On the south-facing wall of the post office, where the half-blind tails of the alleys divide because our streets don't start or finish, someone had written: **CANTON OF CAPITULATION**.

That wall is warm in winter and pleasant in summer, so widows lean their lower backs and narrow hunched shoulders and, under their dark clothes, their still firm little bums against the graffiti.

In my early childhood our old great-grandmother protected that canton. *The insatiable one*, the oldest woman in the world. She was antique all our lives and old for almost half of hers. That day, when she capitulated, the old lady ate a whole plateful of little bitter fish and sweet white cabbage, I recall; the fish were bitter because of their innards, the cabbage was sweet because of the salt in the soil or because of the sun. Then – trying to control the trembling of her chin – out of which coiled several white hairs – she dragged a stool to the end of the road where the widows with dry mouths sat under the yellow neon sign of the new post office, chewing the cud. Some of them spent their last forty years at that corner, some spent forty days, but in the end, sooner or later, they all came, those with black headscarves and those with red pearls. They sat on little benches and spent the whole afternoon saying nothing in their brilliant dialect.

'Cul-de-sac,' Herr Professor would say. Blind alley.

The old men didn't dally in that district – they just waved briefly and moved on – they occupied themselves at the other end of the Settlement, behind the *Illyria* and the slipway. The public social life of pensioners was strictly divided into female and male, as in a boarding school. The men played chess or cards at a long pine table or just sat, talking loudly. On the table's concrete supports, someone had long ago written **TABLE OF LIES**.

Spat at, laughed at, then the next day patted on the back and celebrated, the knights of the Table of Lies, senile amateur politicians with a heart attack in their chests, moved figures of horses and huntsmen with their arthritic fingers, lost castles and pawns and exchanged an oral history of wars, fishing and tourist sex. Demonstrating, proving that the past endures, that everything that once happened goes on simultaneously, and that in fact only the imperfect tense exists – that perfect verbal era and that thin, little borderline of shining conditionals: what would have happened if, a border stretched to infinity between the pluperfect and the future perfect, I reflected.

In former times, the lads from the Old Settlement who were going off to the Yugoslav National Army used to write their names on the walls of their houses, their date of birth and year they were called-up. And they added some well-known lines of verse. At the bus station was written **WAIT FOR ME SELENA** from some song or other.

All these inscriptions became toponyms.

People say: 'Let's meet at Call-up '65' or 'Saw 'im this morning passing the Table of Lies' or 'Wait for me at Selena'. By now the words have been largely washed away by rain and sun – people are beginning to forget why the building with shutters the colour of cornflowers, near the bus station, is called Selena.

The best known of all the graffiti in the Old Settlement was written along the whole length of the parapet at the Main Jetty. It was the spectacle of our childhood – greasy black letters on the white windbreak: **STRANGER, THE LAW DOES NOT PROTECT YOU HERE**. And high up on a mast, at the peak of the windbreak, on one leg stood not a vulture, a scavenger, but a seagull, a scrounger, Martin. All tame seagulls here are called Martin.

Legend has it that this graffito was the work of the Iroquois Brothers, which is impossible – I think that the inscription on the Jetty was quite a lot older than the oldest of them.

In any case, when the waterfront was renovated a dozen years ago, they demolished the whole jetty, stone by stone. Afterwards they put all those large stone blocks back, creating a new windbreak so that you could only make out here and there scattered parts of letters from which it was impossible to read **STRANGER, THE LAW DOES NOT PROTECT YOU HERE**. But then again, that graffito is forever inside, preserved in a sense.

An indelible mark was also left by the unknown hero who wrote, in bright blue paint, all over the Settlement and down in the Centre: *I LOVE YOU, NEDA. AND LOTS MORE BESIDES*.

Just to be sure, he marked several of the more prominent places also with: *HEY, NEDA, DO YOU READ BLUE GRAFITTI?*

And there wasn't a single Neda in the Settlement, just three Nadas. I wondered whether it was meant for one of them, and which.

Then, for a while, there was nothing new on the walls. If you don't count the time when someone poured black paint over the plaque in the Community Hall listing the names of local Partisans and drew a swastika underneath it, and the following night the Partisan statues outside the primary schools and secondary school had their heads taken off. People all muttered about the Iroquois Brothers again, but I think that the business with the bronze heads was carried out by people from the new not yet completed, three-storey buildings on the other side of the railway. 'Neo-outliers', my sister called them. But maybe it wasn't them maybe I'm mistaken. Except in one thing: the Iroquois Brothers were vermin, even when they grew up, but they were too clever to destroy monuments.

In the Settlement there was no war in the sense of shooting; Yugoslav National Army ships fired at the western part of the town for two weeks, and then stopped. From time to time there'd be an air-raid siren, as well. We were 'cut off like on a lilo with sharks circling round it,' said Herr Professor.

My sister said 'there was a stench'. Fear stinks, especially in shelters.

Some young guys from the Old Settlement, several years older than us, died in the war. We all cried.

Some other local men were taken away and disappeared without trace. We were all silent.

Some of our friends and their parents left the Settlement over-night and never came back.

We kids shouted 'Serbian pervert!' to each other. Even the Serbs shouted that, those that hadn't fled during the war or the hostile years that followed.

Everyone talked about snipers, and Mariana Mateljan, who had a personal demon in her head making her a target, arrived from the centre in her orange *Lada*, drenched in sweat from holding her foot on the accelerator, and shouted from the doorway: 'Give me sugar and water! What a dog's life?! Like I was driving soup in a shallow dish!' I recall. But I've forgotten quite a lot.

At that time, since we're discussing graffiti, a big-eared U for the fascist Ustasha regime sprang up for the most part in the centre as a popular design on street wallpaper. Some people did it for a joke, some out of conviction, some as an initiation ritual, and everyone out of boredom.

As far as the monuments went, the worthy citizens used to erect new totems and idols to replace the old ones, in a generational exchange of heroes.

For several days the papers chewed over the case of the name of the waterfront in the Old Settlement: should it be Jere Botušić (fighter in the National Liberation War, b. 1921 – blown to bits by a hand grenade, 1943) Promenade or should the name be changed to Jere Botušić (Croatian defender, b. 1969 – shot to pieces by a shell in 1993) Promenade. In the end a new inscription was placed on the waterfront with the name: Jere Botušić Promenade.

And the days passed peacefully, the walls were silent, the heads of the old statues sunk in the shifting bottom of the sea were silent, and indeed the new statues were silent too, guessing that it was just a matter of time before they too lost their heads.

Of the remaining graffiti of interest to me, there is one up by the railway track, in the little building that was once a waiting room and now serves as a shit-house – an unofficial WC. It's a drawing of a young, smiling, freckled cowboy, riding, instead of a bareback thoroughbred mare, an old bike, 50cc, towards the setting sun. Underneath, it says:

DANIEL R.I.P. THAT'S WHERE COWBOYS GO.

I've learned something about simultaneity: that memory is the present of all remembered events. The tape rolls forward and backwards. Fw-stop-rew-stop-rec-play-stop, it stops at important places, some images flicker dimly frozen in a permanent pause, unclear. But memory is also the saboteur editor in the back room, cutting and pasting, reframing to the every end, or at least until Alzheimer's.

'The past is never completed, obviously,' Herr Professor announces, taking a VHS cassette out of an ancient video player. Only in the Old Settlement are there still people using video players.

'The past isn't what it was,' I said.

That was all that was left of my brother, of his games, this pathetic Herr Karlo, I reflected. He placed his large misshapen mitts on the little garden table, among the porcelain crockery. Like on my brother's skinny shoulders.

'Gingernut,' that's what he called him in the film.

We were there, at the waterfalls on the Krka river, on an excursion that I had entirely wiped from my memory. *Here's my gingernut*, says the vet on the film we had just watched together.

Gingernut and a large hand on the back of his neck, the fingers wrapped in little rusty flames.

Shit, maybe he really did do that with Daniel, I reflected.

I imagined him falling prostrate in front of Daniel, on the cold floor with its mosaic of Chinese tiles, spattered with cat's and dog's blood, and taking out of his jeans' fly with his fat fingers Daniel's proud and indifferent penis.

In the terrarium the lizards fidget, in the formalin, the salamanders float, and the crocodile slaps its tail against the cabbage tub.

Herr Karlo trembles like a bashed cymbal.

After the next cymbal blow (it's a nice day and a holiday, but a filthy grey nimbus has sailed up from the west), together with the lame horns and shrill trumpet, other sounds begin to enter: a mobile ring-tone, the church, a muffled miaowing from the street, the calling and shrieking of a grasshopper which Ma is beating with a twig of tamarisk and loudly cursing its mother. I always return to reality with some invested effort, as though from a distance.

Even if they call me at eleven in the morning or six in the evening, people ask me: Did I wake you? Because that's how I sound. I was awake, of course. I hadn't even been asleep, I reflected.

In reality there exists that almost unreal letter chafing me in my pocket, of that I am certain.

'Mr Šain,' I say in an unfamiliar voice.

Here, in the courtyard, enclosed in high stone walls, where the light is soft, transparent, for an instant I feel (mistakenly) that I have finally, after many years, sat down beside water.

He hasn't heard me. The bell in the tower is ringing more loudly – for St Fjoko – and over the top of the carob tree, crammed with black fruits, I see the turquoise of the sky being squeezed out by the dense evening indigo.

'I need to ask you something.'

'Dada, my dear?'

'Did Daniel ever contact you, after you went away, did he send you any message, letter, email, did he ever get in touch?'

The catfish twitches, barely perceptibly.

Then, as though to himself: 'Why are you tormenting yourself with this? He's no longer here, you have to think of the living – yourself, your mother.'

'It's better not to know some things,' said Ma, and look where her desire not to know has got her. That's what I think, saying nothing.

He pulls out a used handkerchief with a blue edge and blows his nose loudly.

'Why, how would he have found me, I kept moving, from Brela to Rotterdam and then... No, I was all over the place, until I completely ran out of money. I was even, I was even robbed, yes.'

'What about email?'

'I don't know,' he shrugs his shoulders and returns my gaze. 'I rarely use it, if I have to,' he says. 'I've got a bit old,' he says and smiles somewhat bitterly.

The tortoises have separated and are now at two different ends of the garden. They hardly move. What are the chances of them never finding each other again?

'I'd never have done anything to hurt him. It may seem strange to you now, because Dani was almost a child, and I am, obviously, already almost an old man, but he was my best friend.'

As he speaks, the huge man quivers, closes his eyes and opens them wide, swallowing air:

'The fact that he got involved with some lads, a gang, you may know that...

... I warned him, that's not the right company for you...

... He didn't come back here again, anyway...

... They don't like being lectured...

... Perhaps I could have done more...

... I always wonder...

... I could have done more...

... After that, I don't know...

... In any case, you know what happened to me before I left, I was beaten up, half to death, for God's sake...'

As he speaks, he clasps his large hands like a sick person suffering from some acute physical discomfort.

A few unexpected large drops of rain tinkle onto the crockery and drive the magic scarab beetle out of its hiding place under a plate. It stops on the white tablecloth like a forgotten amulet.

'Dung-beetle,' the vet comments drily.

'Yes,' I reply briefly.

My throat is constricted, as though he has stuffed it with those dirty, crusty rags, now dripping on the washing line before our eyes.

'It must be hard for the rain, once it starts, to stop. It would be for me. Like when you're a child and pee in your sleep, without feeling shame or stopping,' says Karlo Šain.

We're protected by the tree-top and the porch, while beyond us it's pouring.

I think fleetingly that Ma has probably not taken the shoes off the steps and now they're getting wet.

I feel the piece of paper in my pocket, the envelope with the stamp; the image of Laika and postmark Perm – where's that and why there – typewritten, a letter that was late and arrived after Daniel's death. If I got it out now, would Karlo Šain say it was his?

He would, I think, and I push the envelope under the tray on the table. Let him find it.

If this reply exists, there must also be a letter that preceded it. I've waited for four years for Herr Professor and that letter of Daniel's, or email, whatever, his voice. And Karlo Šain says it doesn't exist, that Daniel's letter doesn't exist. He looks me in the eye, lying. And mumbles about the rain.

Prof Šain says no letter of any kind ☹. I send my sister a message later.

Reply: *What did I tell you! Leave him be. Who knows who wrote the letter.*

For a time I look blindly at the screen, peed on by the downpour.

Like hell there's no letter. And he's the one. What other idiot would still use a typewriter.

Yet another one of those hottest and longest summers in our lives – the last pre-war one. The sea blossomed and during the day the heat made it stink horribly of decay and sulphur, so during that whole unbearable time we bathed only at night in twinkling phosphorous.

Our father died at the beginning of August. It was the summer in the middle of which our time snapped and became forever unstuck, divided into before and after. It was impossible to put that broken, scattered time back together, or even connect its parts, which is what I keep trying to do.

During those days, the song of billions of cicadas and grasshoppers was transformed into a steady sound that stupefied, into afternoons that boiled noisily and into nocturnal effervescence. Our father told us that if you woke up early enough and went down to the sea, you could hear the seaweed cracking and emitting from its wounds a sticky juice like honey.

'They use it to sweeten tea and spicy foods in Mexico,' he said.

That man had learned everything he knew about the world beyond the Settlement from films.

They sent him home from hospital three weeks ago. He is dying in the big double bed, in the light, airy room on the first floor. If I wake at night, I can hear his alveoli wheezing, his lungs separating and a poisonous sticky juice like honey leaking into the cavities.

My father's window, full of sky, is the only one in the house that looks out onto Long Street. Today is St Fjoko's Day, the town feast-day, and on the corner table are pieces of used cotton wool and a dish of dewy figs.

This is the feast-day, when trombones, a bassoon and cymbals sound, tables and chairs are taken out onto the square and in front of houses.

In the evening, fraternities, Fjokans, put on the specially adorned robes of their brotherhood with hoods and an embroidered gold and scarlet badge on their chests and process one after the other behind the cross-bearer, behind two candle holders, behind the little silver box on a brocade cushion.

After them come nuns and women from the Choir of St Lisa, singing 'Christ on the Beach' and other such hymns. Their freshly shaved husbands carry large candles that sway, so they look like the burning masts of foreign yachts down in the Little Lagoon. Male aromas of incense and Pitralon spread around.

The largest candle, the Leader, was supposed to be carried by our father, but that's impossible because of his illness and imminent death. Death has settled behind his pillow like the monkey, disguised, I could see.

Daniel had gone regularly, almost every day, to the fraternities and asked to be the one to carry it, but the Fjokans said he wasn't strong enough and that 'he should definitely come back in two or three years time'. In the end they gave in, nevertheless.

It was carried in seven circles, up and down, then down and up Long Street. When he couldn't do any more, a large man would take the candle over, that's what the men from the fraternity arranged, Daniel said.

'I'll manage six,' said Daniel seriously. Ma was angry; she thought it was a bad idea.

'Maybe all seven!' he said to me and my sister, later.

They were hot days when the algae were blooming, in which the world as we had known it broke away from our future like part of the Red Sea on the poster for 'The Ten Commandments' on the wall of Braco & Co, while we stayed for a little longer in between, on dry land, perplexed, but careless, cheerful and foolish.

That morning, on St Fjoko's Day, I cut my hair.

Little flame by little flame, the breadbasket filled with fire and when Jill went to sleep in it, I saw that our fur coats were the same, of a similar colour and softness.

This was no ritual, but just a case of 'putting the moment into practice', as Daniel would say – and I don't think it had the slightest connection with what happened later. But it gave me the idea, I recall.

I was still a boy in those days. It was only the following year that my boobs began to grow. (For the rest of the summer, the girls from the Red Cross holiday home would whistle after me in the street and sometimes I liked it, and sometimes I didn't).

I stood for a long time in front of the mirror in Daniel's room in the Fjokans' festive costume, with the hood over my eyes: I'm taller than my brother, but not much, enough – I calculate. And similar, if I drop my shoulders like this and arrange my arms. And my hips, I observed.

* * *

'You can't be the captain,' Daniel said yesterday, as we were sailing on the dysentery sea. He was holding a palm-branch oar, I had the plastic one from the blow-up boat.

'Captainess!' I shrieked.

'You don't get it, there's no such thing. a captain, a cowboy or a woman priest, they don't exist,' he shrugged his shoulders. 'What can I do,' he said, smiling, and I recall, he had a tooth missing.

'What about Calamity Jane?' I yelled fiercely.

He thought for a moment.

'She turns into an ordinary lady in the end.'

I love the scene in which Calamity Jane appears at the top of the stairs in a dress and Wild Bill Hickock falls in love with her – I could rewind it and watch it for hours. He knows that, he's teasing me. I gave him a shove with my oar so that he fell into the sea and I paddled to the shore.

That same afternoon I crept into his room: Indian patchouli sticks were burning to disguise the cigarette smoke. I smoked in the mirror under James Coburn and Kris Kristofferson from 'a stupid, boring male story' as I told Daniel. I had a bit of a rummage through his things, and then picked up the tidily laid out Fjokan costume, put it on and strutted about a bit.

Then, in front of the mirror it struck me. Why not? Something nice and warm rolled up to me and spread through the room. Why not?

'Biiii-iiitch!' yelled Daniel, a little later, down in my room, locked in. 'I'll mur-der you! Honest to God!'

In vain, my room was in the cellar, deep in the rocks, in the house's subconscious. I was sorry for my brother and felt disobedient, but not afraid. The Fearless Rusty.

The joy that buoys me up is strongest. It's called excitement, a warm, golden ball in the belly and lower down, outside me. Like waking again and again. I'll make it through all seven circles. It'll be remembered. Oh, yes.

'Bravo, good for you,' I thought people's eyes were saying in the procession.

'Bravo, Daniel, good lad, well done,' the dumb Fjokans would say afterwards.

My body aches, everything in it hurts, every muscle and nerve, but the joy that buoys me up is far stronger. Behind the cross-bearer with the cross, behind the two candle-holders, behind the little silver box on the brocade cushion.

When we passed my father's window for the fourth time, I summoned the strength to raise my head and look up: I wanted him to see me, and recognize me. He would be surprised, I imagined, and then he would burst out laughing. That was the scenario.

But the window was empty – a breeze had got up, so the blind was down.

The bells rang out again, and the greasy wax Leader slipped through my wet hands and broke dully on the ground.

At the top of the steps, in front of the door, my sister met me with red eyes and slapped me suddenly, palm open, on the cheek: 'You've shorn yourself, you goat!'

From the bedroom we heard my mother's thin squeal and the monkey slunk cackling through the open door, without anyone seeing it, apart from me and ginger Jill.

I broke away and ran after it down the hill to Long Street, towards the castle, though the lanes and dark vaults, to the slipway.

In the dusk, the procession was still milling about like ants when you tread on their anthill. They had stuck the Leader together with isolating tape, I observed from round the corner where I'd hidden. The monkey had crept where it was safest, among people, and vanished in the crowd under the wide skirt of one of the nuns, I saw.

I crawled unseen through the long empty rows of benches and white plastic tables on the square.

Down at the slipway, I'll find Daniel who has forgiven me.

'Sorry,' I'll say. And it'll be sorted.

There he is, my brother: he's picking up seagull feathers for an Indian headdress, and we barely hear the sound of a departing ambulance.

4

Every day I say I'm looking for work and then I go wandering. Although no one expects me to get a job: my sister acquired a sharp tongue, my brother a silver Colt, while I acquired my father's pension in order to carry on studying. But I didn't feel like learning anything any more, not in school.

'You just be yet another stupid character in the Croatian novel,' my sister snapped.

She doesn't understand. She studied at home, worked and took all her exams on time, I know. Whenever I mention abandoning my degree, she looks at me the way one looks at a lost cause or an incomprehensible object. Which is, truth to tell, ontologically speaking the same thing, I reflected.

I had left Zagreb behind me as the most faraway city on earth, further than Osaka and Juneau and Santa Fe.

'That's what the towns where you abandon your failed illusions are like,' Ned Montgomery would say, riding off into the sunset with a cigarette between his teeth. Ned Montgomery is a romantic cowboy after all.

'I can't imagine going back to that city.'

'Your call, but it's the only quasi-city in this wasteland,' said my sister, brushing the hair out of my eyes.

'Karlo Šain says it's all the same thing, that our mentality can be described in four words, from *you never will* in the south to *whatever* in the north,' I said.

'Really?!' said my sister, looking at me in surprise. She didn't know I'd already been to the Professor's. 'Well, the old pervert's right. From arrogant mules in the south to haughty fools in the north. However much you shift the crap and carrion around in this sewer, as soon as you raise your head, it floats into your mouth.'

'And so, what you gonna be when you grow up?' she asked, lighting a thin white cigarette. The stain on the filter was greasy and the dark colour of sour cherries. That lipstick suits her best, I reflected.

I shrugged my shoulders. I could be a writer, get into the papers, but my stories are shit, or I'll start a village business, go into agriculture, I reflected. There must be some state incentives for that, It's quite popular.

'You'll never be staying in the Old Settlement?' my sister asked in an anxious tone, dusting the non-existent dandruff from my shoulders. 'Small places is good while you're small. Later they cut you down to their own size.'

'Maybe I'll go to Mehico after all,' I sighed. 'I'm already learning: hasta luengo, amigos! Bienvenida estranjera!'

I had learned that from the soaps Ma watches.

Speaking of Mexico, since I'd come home, I had tried several times to get in touch with my former room-mate, but she had left Zagreb too. Everyone was forever on the move; everyone was looking for something, stumbling about, all chasing their tails.

Afterwards she phoned from Berlin, from a *Tex-Mex* restaurant. Her old man had withdrawn her from her law course, after she'd flunked the fourth year for a second time.

'Guess what, Dada,' she said, 'I've become vegan! I've spent the whole summer shovelling gristle rissoles around on a hotplate. Meat makes me gag.'

At one time her old man in Berlin had owned one of those Croatian restaurants that serve Balkan stew and charcoal grilled food, but he had recently moved over to Mexican.

'You're late again, old man, it's Japanese eateries that are in now – sushi, saki, shitake,' my room-mate told him, but her father responded by 'nearly clipping me round the ear.'

'Send Ma to me for a month's rehab, we'll sort her out,' she said.

'Big deal,' she said, 'it's like getting off poke-balls. Poke-balls for me, pills for her, isn't that right?' she said from her mobile.

On the screen was her face from her emo-phase with a tongue stud. Before that she'd had a neo-punk phase, and a hippy one at high school. She'd passed through all these trends as through a chain of clothes stores.

'I'm the last emo-girl,' she'd concluded while we were still in Zagreb.

'You're certainly the oldest emo-girl, and probably the last,' I said.

I imagined her as a little old Gothic lady, but little old ladies, at least the ones here in the Settlement, are generally Gothic in any case, that's their dress code.

My room-mate and my Ma would get on well, I reflected. They could go to the graveyard together and shave their heads in keeping with the *Weltschmerz*.

I'm thinking as though *she* had settled in my head, I reflected, immediately afterwards, anxiously. I really am my sister's sister.

Sar-cas-ti-cal-ly, I reflected, in syllables.

Perhaps my sister is in my head like a *Cymothoa exigua*, a parasite that the vet Karlo Šain had once shown me – it eats a fish's tongue and then stays in its mouth forever, in its place.

'Hasta luengo, estranjera,' I said to my room-mate at the end of our conversation.

'Huh?' she said.

'Farewell, stranger – I learned that from the soaps Ma watches. What d'you think, maybe I could be an actress?' I said.

'Like hell!' she said. 'Ha ha ha,' she said, 'just kidding. Don't forget, Dada – all famous actors were first waiters or else they were photographed nude.'

For the first time in my life, something is happening in the Old Settlement: half the population is dressed in denim and gingham because of Montgomery's film, everyone's involved.

The shooting is to last about a month: round the tents and pre-fabricated huts a whole small garden has sprung up with paprika, camomile and marijuana plants.

Cursed Rider, that's what the film's called. Couldn't they have thought of a cleverer name than *Cursed Rider*, I thought, anxiously. There's a whiff of trash about it.

'Bet it's about vampires,' said my sister when she heard. 'Everything's about vampires these days.'

'What kind of vampires d'you get in a Western?' I asked.

'Handsome,' she said.

'It's the eclecticism of the early twenty-first century, anything goes,' she said.

'What's that?' I asked.

'Bosnian stew that's trying to be moussaka, probably,' she said.

'Tutti frutti gelato?!'

'Don't be so fucking benign.'

During those days, wandering along the edge of summer, before my final decision to leave the Old Settlement and before the cooling soil had finally lapped up all the velvety, russet and gold juice of September, I at last met Angelo in the prairie, beyond the railway track.

There's something about beautiful people that suggests a deceptive good fortune, I feel that when I happen to meet them in passing, it's a joy for the eye that it's easy to get used to. I can't say that beautiful people particularly appeal to me or that they particularly attract me, but I like their beauty.

For a time, when I was a child, I used to stay after class sitting in front of the primary school until our Italian language teacher came past. I had never before met a girl who looked like that or dressed like that; sometimes I waited for an hour or two just for her to pass and say hello to me.

Later my idols were less beautiful, very often even ugly, but Angelo was someone I wanted to look at. Not as an idol, but the way, from time to time, some men look at me.

People said that during the war his father had sent him to America. He's got an aunt there, they said. As soon as he had grown up, he was taken in by a lady who found him in the street.

'How did he end up there?' I asked the people who were telling me, but they just shrugged their shoulders and stabbed at a few guesses. The journey from the well-heated home of some mother or aunt to the street seemed unbelievably long, but 'mostly it's enough just to open the door,' they said.

'While he was on the street he learned to play the mouth organ and ocarina really well! And some other things too!' they said, grinning conspiratorially and as though they had long ago solved every rebus puzzle.

In previous summers Angelo used sometimes to play on the *Illyria* summer terrace and Mariana Mateljan said that some foreign women ('in their prime,' said Mariana Mateljan), used to offer him money and their life for a little tenderness and sometimes he took both.

As I rode my moped along the stream towards the cabbage fields and olive groves behind which the film everyone was talking about was being shot, I already knew that I was actually looking for him. If I hadn't known, it was perfectly clear as soon as I set eyes on him.

He was sitting on the ground, against a wall, beside a pile of truck tyres, playing a comb.

I don't know what I could say about that particular skill, but it couldn't be said that it didn't suit him.

I pushed my bike straight up to the pile of tyres, kicked its stand down and said:

'Hey, ciao.'

'What?'

'*For a Dollar More?*' I asked, partly to show I was in the swing, because I knew that was the theme. To be honest, there aren't many tunes for the comb, at least not as far as I know.

'Yep,' he said, carrying on playing. 'Morricone.'

I hadn't impressed him.

'You're Rusty,' he said, looking me up and down.

His tuxedo was dusty, under it was the bare torso of a golden lad and round his neck was a white silk scarf. Seen from close up it was obvious that he was a little peacock, he couldn't be more than twenty.

'I knew your brother,' he said and spat on a bug crawling in the dust, quite accurately.

Usually people don't say that, I reflected, usually they don't mention Daniel to me, *they are careful* about that.

In his yellow eyes Angelo has a black spark, on his short boots spurs for the requirements of the film, I observed. On the spurs, appropriately a star; and on his Adam's apple, quite inappropriately, a drop of dark sunlight.

'So, you act?' I asked, and spat as well, it just came over me. That explains why he goes around in these clothes.

'You could say I act. But I don't say anything, just play music,' he said, scratching his dark chin.

'I've been sort of thinking about becoming an actress,' I said frivolously. 'But I've given up the idea. The ideal thing seems to me to travel round the world, writing tourist guides. Can you believe that there are lucky guys who do that for a living!?'

'Oh,' he said seriously, 'I think you could be whatever you want.'

What does he mean by that *whatever you want*, I wondered. Presumably that's something good, I reflected; a compliment, maybe.

'How do you know Daniel?' I asked.

'I didn't know him that well, just from the street, you know,' he frowned. 'Sorry.'

'It's OK,' I said. 'It was me who asked.'

The prairie is beautiful at this time of year. In summer no one feels like farming, so it's all overgrown with tall dry grasses stretching all the way to Majurina, to the three-storey building with no façade, where Maria Čarija and her relatives, their children, dogs, hens and goats live. In front of their building and the houses some hundred metres away where their close kin, a whole tribe, live, there's no longer a single blade of grass. Vegetables and fruit do badly, they say that Majurina is a sand bar, left when the sea retreated and that everything drains away through that soil. The Iroquois have a small herd of goats, which have of necessity become fairly independent and take care of themselves. Those goats sometimes climb trees to browse on the leaves, and that's quite a scene – as though goats were growing on the trees.

Some of the actors went up to the houses and wanted to take photographs of them, but the 'Iroquois Brothers' weren't thrilled at the idea,' said Angelo, laughing. The drop of light jiggled on his throat.

The strangest thing about a man's body has always seemed to me his Adam's apple. But his was acceptable.

'Come with me, I'll show you everything,' my harmonica-man beckoned me and I followed him, his boyish nape, the curls on the back of his head, his arms, shoulders, back, his small muscular bum, his downy bare ankles, his voice of soft cotton, with deeper tones. What flickered in his vocal chords echoed deep in my belly and between the fingers I had thrust into my pockets.

The insatiable one had talked about love as a sudden thunder-clap. 'Colpo di fumine,' she used to say. What would she say about Angelo if she could see him?

'Handsome as an actor,' my great-grandmother would say.

'Shame he's a tart,' my sister would say.

'Love is over-estimation of the sexual object,' Freud would say.

Maybe I'm falling in love again, I reflected anxiously.

He turned round to check that I was following him.

There were some interesting objects on the set. Colourful as a circus, a whole world within another, and both of them in a third; horses, cameras, and people.

I glanced all around to see whether I could catch a glimpse of Ned Montgomery.

I imagine the cowboy as he is on the poster in my bedroom – a tough guy of unshakeable resolve with a cobalt gaze and eye-brows of wire, a great white hero. Although, to be honest, in all the more recent pictures in the newspapers he's already old and crumpled, with a very red neck.

'He doesn't come here,' said Angelo.

'They say he was a great actor,' he added.

'Right,' I nodded. 'For some, maybe the greatest.'

Hen-extras of various colours were wandering about, so the trampled, scorched grass was full of chicken shit. I kicked several little balls away with the tip of my trainer.

'The Indians use it to make us tea,' said Angelo, squinting unobtrusively at my boobs, I observed.

'Oh sure,' I said for the sake of saying something. He laughed again, displaying his teeth, small and white, like milk teeth.

In front of one tent sat a magnificent witch doctor resembling an extinct bird with yellow, red and white feathers. a gloomy, proud wizard, a priest of flora and fauna. 'Oniric being,' my sister would say.

'That's the old Gippo, the one who begs round the boutiques,' said Angelo.

She appears in one scene as the tribal witch-doctor, he explained. Her heavy feathered headdress rests on her shoulders, a shawl like wings, she has a red mark on her forehead.

'Let's 'ave a look,' said the Gypsy as soon as I approached, taking my hand and looking at my palm. I drew it back and shoved it into my pocket.

'The Gippo doesn't have panties under her skirts and if no one gives her anything in a shop, she stands on the threshold and pees down her legs, as though it's nothing to do with her,' Daniel had once said, I recalled. But now she was wearing trousers. Her great, luxuriant tits were confined in a richly embroidered waistcoat.

'You 'ave night in your soul, I can read that from your brow,' the Gypsy told me crossly and spat into the dust.

'You guessed right,' I said and put both hands on my hips. 'But I have a warm and sunny heart,' I said, as a joke and because of Angelo.

Her eyes widened – two drops of pitch – then narrowed to dark spark.

'Well, you may 'ave a 'eart, but if you 'ave a heart, you can't 'ave panties,' said the Gypsy wizard, dragging her feathers of Paradise through the dust among the sparrows and scavengers.

The sun was now high above us, but its metal glare was softened by the approaching autumn. Some stars from the soaps that Ma watches emerged from the wigwams, I recognized them. They greeted Angelo. We walked along beside the façade of a building made of plasterboard and plywood, somewhere in the Wild West.

My new friend was in a good mood, my words stuck in my throat.

'You've got something here,' removing an insect from my T-shirt.

He did that on purpose, I reflected. We were sniffing each other like two Spaniel puppies, one red, one black. Any minute now, our tongues will start lolling.

'Come on, angel, take out your harmonica and play me something,' called an actor. I recognized him from a children's programme.

Our attention was drawn to a cloud of dust out of which emerged a cabriolet – the young lady in the light-coloured suit, this time with her hair down and dark glasses on her face. The one who had picked him up that afternoon when I was watching them from my window. She gestured to him, pushing her dark glasses up. The boy stirred lazily, put his comb into his back pocket and strolled towards her.

Damnation, they would say in a Western.

'Ah, damnation, what can you do,' I said to my little motorized pony, watching the tall, handsome young man walking away from me, without ever having been mine.

Tame as a little dog, I reflected sadly.

I had the impression they were arguing, so I sparked the bike and sped off along the tarmac. I didn't have much appetite for marital or non-marital scenes, and besides, there was an important errand I had to make.

Behind the tents, the extras were drinking coffee that they poured from a thermos flask into cups – I observed – and the Gipsy, laying her feathers down beside her on a chair, read their fortunes in the grounds.

Several hens squawked when I revved the bike.

Through the window of the red car, in my rear mirror, Billy the Kid kissed his tanned sponsor.

I dashed through the early dusk towards the Last Chance, following the smooth curves of its neon aura. In front of me, in the distance above the wood, the skeletons of cranes loomed over the hill and high-rise buildings. My tyres crunched on fir-cones scattered over the ground by the night wind – a loud summer wind that drove me to go faster. Inland the wind has no sharpness, it excites you softly, but when I slow down, I can hear the rigging jangling on the masts down in the harbour and ships howling through their halyards.

The *Last Chance* is a place with a reputation: good and bad. Its dark door always swallows us gladly and afterwards spits us, communicants, out into the calmer night.

Dutch Sonja opened this dive in the middle of the nineteen-eighties in a copse beside the sea, in Kućica – an abandoned beach complex below the former Red Cross rest home, halfway between the Settlement and the town centre, on the shore. The place became famous because it stayed open until 4 am, when everything else was closed.

As children, we rarely went into that pinewood; by day a local exhibitionist tended to roam around there, and at night there was no lighting.

'Wanker', that's what we called them, those exhibitionists. There were two or three of them in the Settlement, and the girls used sometimes to see them in the company of their fathers or brothers, in cafés or garages. So the girls generally said nothing about it. Sometimes the wankers were their fathers or brothers. I knew four sisters who had a house beside a stream, below the highway. The oldest would blush whenever she saw us, even at school, she was always red in the face, that little girl we called Karolina-the-wanker's-daughter, casually, as though we were saying Karolina the postman's or the dentist's daughter or Karolina of Monaco.

There's something suppressed about the Old Settlement, 'like venereal disease on the brain,' said my sister.

'Like *Twin Peaks*?' I asked, while my stomach gave a lurch backwards, as when I was a child.

The innocent and God-fearing Old Settlement, at the time of plant spraying, at the time of the intensive evaporation of smells, stank and crackled like a red-hot cod fish in a pan.

'Man,' said my sister, 'sometimes I think no one here fucks naturally or without a pang of conscience.'

'Catholicism in the Balkans, think about it, what a combination, that simply has to be perversion to the nth degree,' she said.

But people do fuck, because the streetlights never work, I reflected. The attempts to fix them were a serial fiasco, because some sensitive lover would always throw a stone from a copse and break the bulb. The only light was the neon coconut palm at the *Last Chance*, flickering on the deserted island of sighs, in the middle of the indigo night. The *Chance* changed its owners, closed, but in the end always re-opened the entrance into its deep maw with the bright pink tongues of light reaching out from inside. For every lost creature on the road. For all of us.

I left the moped unchained outside the door and bowled in along with the wind. The little house immediately licked its lips.

From the doorway, I caught sight of the short figure with the baseball cap I was looking for. His short legs, out of proportion to his body-built torso and round head, were swinging comically from the bar stool. He was sitting at the poker apparatus, pressing a red button with two fingers of one hand.

'Ahoy, long time no see,' the man at the bar winked by way of a greeting and gestured with his chin towards my dealer. 'Hacker,' he said. 'Plays better than the apparatus.'

Diana was smoking and putting clean glasses away.

The queer fellow swivelled on the stool to face me.

'Rusty?! Henry George,' he said, offering me his hand cordially and formally, in the style of a travelling salesman, a young manager. He had glasses with thick lenses, but in fashionable frames, like TV-hosts or teenage rap stars.

His little feet, size thirty-seven, roughly, in high Nike trainers, kept slipping off the footrest and dangling in the air. He was chewing gum; he'd blocked his ears with headphones.

I wouldn't have been surprised if he started offering me porn movies, LSD or decoded mobiles.

'This is my seventh coffee today,' said Henry George, licking his plastic spoon.

'Not good for the stomach,' I said for something to say.

'That's what life's like for us journalists, legend,' said the to-halfway-man from-halfway-child.

His name had been appearing recently on the pages of corporation newsletters, I'd noticed. But any information, or disinformation, could be bought from him in various forms also privately, he was known for that.

'Here's the money, give me the file, and I'm off,' I said.

He thrust a little black stick, with *DataTraveler* written on it under my nose.

'You're jittery... What's the rush, legend?!'

I put the money on the table, picked up the USB stick, nodded to him and left.

'Hey-hey,' I heard a voice behind me in the wood, after I'd already taken a few steps, and was trying to kick-start the engine and leap on – that was an old trick for starting crocks like my bike. The man behind me was Henry George, I knew without looking round, he was coming towards me.

'Hey, legend, you're the first person not to ask me which is my first name and which my surname.'

I shrugged my shoulders.

'I'll buy you a drink.'

'No, thanks. My stomach's not quite right,' I lied.

'No shit? As you like. Well, if you ever need me...'

He made that *call-my-mobile* gesture with raised thumb and crooked little finger. I really hate that so I glowered.

'Hey, legend, don't be mad at me, don't forget you were the one who looked me up,' he said, winking.

'I didn't say anything,' I said.

'Sure, but I get your drift,' he said. 'Always the same, always 'enry the cunt. And who is it I get this shit for, if not for you, fine, honest folk. And what'm I, an ordinary supplier, small-scale merchant. People say, George, oh 'e spreads tales around, sells scandals, dubious type. But I'm a professional, a 'andler. I don't ask superfluous questions, I work to order. If it wasn't me, it'd be someone else, worse, wouldn't it? Private landlord, showman, obliging fixer and bar girl, if you want, that's me, nothing else! But the clientele wants celebrity soup and blood, that's what they say. It's all showbiz. And I do this for fun and dosh. Like everyone else.

You're presumably not so stupid as to think that people do bad things 'cause of some childhood trauma or some ideology, religion, doctrine or mother-fucker? I've got news for you, legend – folk like shit! They're crazy for shit. For instance, people really like to 'ammer someone from time to time. It just comes over them. And if we're being radical, think of wars, when their leash is loosened a bit and it's, like, they're doing it under the patronage of some god-the-father, like, they kill and rape for the 'omeland, church, king, some big wanker. The rabble can't 'ardly wait for a war like a sports match to let off some steam. You don't know who enjoys it more, the one watching and cheering or the one taking part.

And I'm at the end of the food chain, supplier of fast food, courier of the fifth division. D'you want scandal or crime? Crime or scandal?

You see, all these massacres, they're all based on the entertainment industry, the whole thing is one great cheerful scandal, a bit of sex, a little good old 'orror, slitting, screwing and slaughtering. And then 'ere's our controversial 'entry, service on demand. You asked – look! No, legend, no one's even trying to wrap it up nice now. And I'm your waiter, postman, commercial traveller, business-like as a cash-machine, and entertaining as a clown...'

Then he disappeared somewhere behind the pine trees, on the short, swift legs of a dachshund, and with the head of a mole, Morloch – the underground proletarian.

Ma had put on lipstick, found quite a nice old hat of my sister's and, in a green dress full of daylight, she walked to the bus station, touting her straw basket as usual. She wasn't going to the cemetery, she was going 'to see her relative, Mariana Mateljan, to play rummy,' she said. She had turned down the offer of her relative coming for her, although 'she offered several times,' she said. She wanted to walk in the nice weather. I hoped that she wasn't going to one of her doctors – because, I realized, Ma had a whole network of physicians – to replenish her supplies of Normabel and Xanax.

'Mother's an addict ☹', a film trailer would sometimes flash through my head like an axe. Mother's an addict.

'Aha, she's showing signs of life,' commented my sister's voice at the other end of the receiver, munching an apple when I explained where Ma was.

'Well great, that's good news, very.' The apple crunched.

I had the feeling my sister wasn't really listening to me, I heard the sounds of a clicking mouse from the other end.

When she came back from her rummy game at her relative Mariana Mateljan's, Ma looked pleased. Her cards had 'always come out,' she said. She washed her hands with a scrubbing brush, soap and water that steamed; took off her shoes and nylons and shooed ginger Jill out of her armchair with a rolled-up newspaper.

'Psssht,' she said.

The cat opened her glassy emerald eye, got up and curled up a little further away, on the rug under the television.

'You know,' said Ma, hanging her stockings over the back of the armchair, then sitting down, 'at first, after he died, I spent years waitin' for your dad to appear. For the last four years, I've been waitin' for your brother too. I've waited for him every day from dawn to dusk but now I see he won't be comin'.'

Her voice was calm and sure as though she was reading from a book. Her upper lip was sprinkled with moisture, I observed. Perhaps she was ill.

She sat in one of those armchairs of hers, worn by her back and behind, her make-up wiped off and barefoot like an old child, and I was overcome, quite out of the blue, by an unbearable desire to throw a vase or a slipper at her. My eyes, throat and nose suddenly filled with tears. I sat down beside her, on the arm, and thrust the crisps I was eating under her chin. Pizza-flavoured, it said. They tasted of Styrofoam and my saliva.

'What will they think of next,' said Ma, peering into the packet. 'I'll make a real pizza. Tomorrow. With real tomato sauce.'

She had brought two large plastic bags full of firm plum tomatoes from Mariana Mateljan's garden.

I rubbed her elbow, cheeks, the woolly white growth on her nape. I hadn't touched her for years, I reflected; pressing a kiss onto her cold, dry cheek. She still had the same smell of talc. It feels strange to touch Ma, I reflected. It was as though two skinless people were touching.

We sat on the terrace, skinning scalded tomatoes until night fell and our fingers became wrinkled and old.

Two or three drops escaped from my nostrils down my lips, onto the floor and into the dish. Just as well my sister can't see me, I reflected. Crying out of my nose.

Daniel, my brother, died in his eighteenth year, by jumping from a concrete bridge over the railway under a speeding Osijek–Zagreb–Split Intercity train.

He hadn't appeared at school that morning, he had turned off towards the highway, beside the dry stream, then under it through the secret tunnel beneath the road and along the well-known gravel path to the railway, I can imagine it clearly.

At that time, Ma was a cook in the *Illyria* hotel canteen. Until late in the day she made the roux and sauces, instant beef stew and dolce Garbo, which gave our sweetish-sour childhood its aroma. By the time she realized Daniel hadn't come home, her son had been dead for hours.

Two policemen appeared at the door and when Ma opened it, they said: 'Your son so-and-so is dead, he threw himself under a train,' and she slammed the door and called my sister.

'There are a couple of policemen outside, they say that our Daniel has killed himself. Please come and tell them to go away.'

I sometimes pass under that bridge, up and down, I clamber up and look at all that he saw: the housing estate devouring the golden prairie, the olive groves climbing onto the bare hill and the seagulls flying up from the rubbish dumps and from the direction of the slaughterhouse; vineyards spattered with Bordeaux mixture, of a poisonous, childish colour, where dark grapes grow, along with hawthorn bushes full of berries and thorns.

'In Dante's forest of suicides, in the Inferno, their severed limbs, or rather thorny branches, drip blood and words,' said Herr Professor, placing a cup over the scarab beetle, which the large raindrops had frightened and driven under a little china plate. And I tried to imagine my brother as a hawthorn bush I had seen under the bridge. An ordinary thorny bush in the sun: with no blood, without a single word, of course.

There's nothing, that's the worst of it.

Everything's the opposite of what it seems: hell is a comfort to the living, while heaven is ordinary blackmail.

As children we had run across this same railway track innumerable times. We picked the flowers piercing through the stones scattered between the sleepers and brambles in the dry stone wall. The track was our frontier at the time of the wars with the Iroquois, this very place in front of the bridge where the St Andrew's cross is, and the trains whistle as they pass. They were brief battles, attacks from ambush, from behind broom shrubs, mostly without injuries. In times of peace and privilege brought by good weather, we went with our enemies to steal bitter cherries in the fields and searched round the pylon for telephone wires from which we fashioned bullets for catapults or else we made our way down to the cave – the old quarry, to the rubbish tip and found interesting objects and foreign newspapers with wonderful photographs.

'Amazing adverts,' Tomi Iroquois used to say thoughtfully.

So the afternoon would pass.

We would lay our ears on the tracks and listen to hear whether a train was coming. Around us sharp grasses of healing aroma gave off their scent and sunny bumblebees buzzed. Or the prairie lay silent scattered with morning frost.

So the autumn, and winter, would pass.

For the second evening running I go down to that house and sit in the dark in front of it, under the wild fig tree. All the fruit has fallen off and squashed on the stones. The Old Settlement is crammed with that grimy fruit – mulberries, hackberries and figs – which means that the streets are sticky, full of flies and greasy stains.

Over the wall the Šains' old house stares at me. There is nothing left of all the *grandezza* that Mariana Mateljan raves about, apart from glittering fragments of glass on the façade and a few dubious paintings and details like the themes of those little poems with lots of vocatives.

'If there's a reply, there must be a letter that preceded it,' I'll go in and tell him.

'Isn't that letter yours?' I'll say. The letter from Perm, typed on a rickety typewriter.

I'm sitting directly opposite the gate to his courtyard, where it says: *K. Šain Small Animal Veterinary Clinic.*

And it seems to me that the ancient, lop-sided house over the wall is watching me; the half-open senile windows squint at me. In my pocket I have the black stick with the half peeled off label *DataTraveler.* I could aim it at him; I could press it into his temple. Shove it into his mouth. Ask him for whatever he has of Daniel in return for the film.

It's a black stick containing a copy of the amateur porno video, the one I had first seen at that private party in Zagreb. The copy is poor and murky. It had evidently been dark in the room, I reflected. It begins with the expression on the face of the man rearing up over a thin, white body. a young girl or, which seemed more likely, a very young boy, unknown to me. The fucker is holding the object of his lust by the shoulder or neck, a bit too firmly with one hand, with the other he is pressing it slowly downwards, grabbing lower down, pushing in and thrusting slowly and powerfully and crying increasingly loudly until he climaxes, grunting and sobbing. That howling is what it's impossible to forget. That crying was in fact why I had recognized his voice: a deep, but nasal voice, as when a child is trying to imitate an adult man.

'Listen to the old pig squealing!' someone in the room had commented during the projection, laughing, and I shut the door, went out into the street and walked for hours. I walked beside the Sava River, over the dyke and further on, until I collapsed with exhaustion and stayed lying in the mud and grass.

When we had sat in his garden several weeks earlier, the man from the film, whose blurred face I had been reconstructing all these years, the porno star Herr Professor Karlo Šain had said to me, topping up my rose brandy in a glass of the finest crystal: 'I haven't sought or received much in life, dear Dada. And a little radiance would have been enough. You understand, just a fingerful of radiance, something gilded.'

His announcement was accompanied by the cacophony of trombones escaping from the rain. 'I have to go,' I said abruptly. 'The shoes outside our door are getting wet.'

I shoved the envelope with Laika on the stamp under a china dish.

How could someone who wanted something gilded agree so easily to end up in shit? I reflected. And this was a person my brother had trusted. On top of everything else, a liar.

To make matters worse, he had added that the only radiance in his life was Daniel. And then he put his hands over his face as though he was going to sob. Like a pleated fan, I reflected. Oh, damn it all, I thought. But he restrained himself.

Does someone who wants to see radiance look through his own fingers?

The lad, a good-looking young stud with dark hair, the twin brother of that girl from Ipanema, bronzed, slender, manly, smiles, catches me round the waist and, as poems and stories would say, we ride off through the night, over the asphalt, through the dust, under the dense forest of jumbo posters, past the poster of General Gotovina, larger than life, over the bridge, past the industrial zone, past the sign saying Jesus Loves You.

And who wouldn't love you, I reflect.

My bike is a Zippo, it fires in a shudder, abruptly, it stinks of petrol with a bit of octane and burns slowly, my Zippo is an eternal foal, a tin nag, my Boreas, foot-soldier, a 50 cc witch's broom which carries you through my native desert. In a word, my Zippo is a solid scooter, it's not short of breath given that it can carry two young people uphill like this without stumbling.

The short, soft beard of my co-driver tickles my neck, while he laughs into my ear, a soft baritone that reverberates in my ribs, the smell of his white T-shirt... My hair whips his cheeks, and the sandy wind, full of little needles and sea salt, drives tears into his eyes.

We spent the whole night slowly and persistently breaking and opening one another. And now I had buried my face between the boy's relaxed thighs. My mouth feels sour as though I'd been sucking the unripe plums or figs that we picked on the way and ate without peeling. My throat burns with hungrily, greedily swallowed milk, hot and salty. His unruly, forked tongue is now sleeping in my belly button, and I nurse his cock, tender and brown as sugar, darker than his skin, between my palms. Sour milk and sweet flesh, you're sweet and sour, I croon to the sleeping lad, to myself. He's lying propped on his side, his neck curved, his mouth slightly open. He sleeps peacefully, deeply, dreaming of me. My hair slumbers between his thighs wet with kisses, stuck to the thick hairs of his groin. It's not clear exactly where he begins and where I end, our destinies have entwined in the course of one night like the dreadlocks of a little she-devil.

He took the pulp Westerns out of the box that occupies a good part of the space under the bed in the little room. They had lain there, who knows since when, with some cartoons and old cassettes from the Braco & Co video store, which I certainly wanted to look at again, if I could remember where the video player had ended up.

'Daniel's?' he asked.

'As a matter of fact, these were our father's, he really liked those Westerns.'

It was very late, an owl could be heard in the park down the street.

'Have you noticed there haven't been any cicadas this summer?' I said, for the sake of saying something.

'It'll be the spraying, they must have spread something,' he said, handing me the bottle.

'And those are some of his actors?' he asked.

'Huh?'

'Cowboys,' he pointed towards the wall with his chin.

'Yep,' I said, 'Dad's beloved actors. Although they were Daniel's as well.'

Who could explain that.

'Do you recognize anyone?' I asked.

Over my head were two of Clint Eastwood and Franco Nero in *Django* – dragging the muddy coffin behind him – and young Ned Montgomery in *Gold Dust*. He's stepping towards us with a smile in the corner of his mouth and with six shiny Colts under his open bison-skin coat.

'Father loved those spaghetti Westerns, like cartoons or Partisan films, heroes and snappy dressers, lots of bodies, one guy fixes it all. Kill everyone and then come back alone. What's more, he worked in the cinema, before the war, afterwards in the *Braco* video shop.'

I'm burbling, I thought.

He closed his eyes, holding the bottle, nearly empty, against his chest.

'And your old man... why was he so keen on Westerns?'

'No idea, don't remember. They were very popular at the time. Mother says he was naïve. Maybe that's why.'

'He was naïve?'

'Naïve, that's what they say when a man doesn't earn enough to feed his family,' I said.

I went out into the hall and closed the shutters in *the library*, they were half-open, because a warm wind had been drawn into the streets and gusts blew dust and pine needles from the park, rattling against the windowpanes. The little owl was still calling outside and the sea was starting to swell, while the church bell rang once: on the half hour. Half-past two. Upstairs Ma was puffing rhythmically in her cell in a deaf analgesic paradise.

'I think the thing with my father and Westerns had some connection with a higher justice, with the question of honour,' I said coming back into the room, and thinking only how much I wanted to bury my face painlessly in a ball under Angelo's wing; and not to lose him, not to scare him off.

'A question of *honour*?' he laughed, grabbing me by the hand and pulling me to him. Brave, I thought.

'You really are a comical lassie – I haven't heard that word since primary school!'

'Honestly?'

'Yep,' he said.

'Well, that's not very honourable of you, then,' I said.

On his dark arms there is golden, summer fur, silver on the bare, inner side of his forearm, veins and moles, small scratches and scars, skin like the map of a secret country, strong bones in his hands, slender thief's fingers.

I have to lean my face on your belly, touch your tip with the tops of my fingers, and kiss you where it hurts most.

'OK, OK, well done, you won,' he picks up the game, his eyes, teeth and smile sparkle, he pulls me by the fingers a bit closer still, to himself.

'So, who'll do the honours?'

Barefoot like that, beside each other, we are the same height. That unruly blotch of sun, the badge on his Adam's apple, jiggles in his throat.

'You do the honours,' I laugh. 'And I am deeply honoured.'

One night, just one single night in the world, we tenaciously bent and opened one another till morning, and our destinies intertwined like the dreadlocks of a little she-devil. Afterwards we were no longer sure whose hand and whose word was whose. I was to twist that night, which would not be repeated, a thousand times in myself, like a needle in flesh.

When the first light began to creep into the room, he said, 'sleep, Rusty,' turned onto his side and flung his arm closer towards me.

Over a chair in the corner of the room he'd thrown his funny blue tuxedo – you could see it in the dark. It had taken on the shape of his shoulders and arms and when I glanced through my eyelashes in that direction, it seemed as if a wounded animal was breathing at the back of the room.

It's the third evening that I've been going down to the house that watches me over the ramparts, through dozens of invisible vantage points. The hot wind that has managed to seep through the tightly crammed walls raises a flutter from the courtyard and there's no other sound apart from the noise of my blood in my ears.

'Perhaps it will appear strange, dear Dada, but your brother was my best, perhaps even my only friend,' said Karlo Šain.

'The only radiant thing in my life was my friendship with Daniel. He was a radiant person. And a brilliant, talented young man,' he said. 'I would never have hurt him,' he said.

'Do you think an evil person is a sick person, that all his organs are sick. That he has an evil kidney and an evil nail and an evil complexion?' I asked my sister.

My sister made a Nietzsche meets Jesus face and said: 'Even such a person loves someone.'

But Herr Professor is not even evil, I reflected furiously. Just pathetic, I reflected. Pathetic, pathetic, I reflected furiously.

I don't have weapons, strength or power, I just have black mail, black post, a black USB stick.

'Megabytes of shame,' said Henry George, pushing the stick across the table.

I can aim this at the Professor, I can press the stick against his temple, blackmail him.

And what if Karlo starts laughing? What if he doesn't care? What does he have to lose? And what if this, and what if that?

'Cold as snow, you have nerves of steel and you're not afraid,' said an implacable super hero.

'You really could be seventeen,' said a man, placing his wife's pillow under my back.

'I don't know what it is, Dada, but something's not right here,' said my brother Daniel.

'Did you know it's been proved that at the moment of death the brain screams?' I asked the vet Karlo Šain, then, rhetorically, in his garden, between two mouthfuls of cake. And I scream, like a fucked-up puppet that has been exposed for too long to a house of horrors, until it turns bad. I scream, noiselessly and suddenly. Screaming in my head happens to me like hiccups or belching does to other people.

Blackmail, black mail, black post, a black stick, and black clefts in the manhole under my feet.

And what if this, and what if that?

'A pistol is good or bad, like the man who carries it,' said Shane in my head. Oh, Shane, get lost, I think. I crouch down and throw it in: the Data Traveller with its peeling label travels along the smelly underground channel out of which – thanks to the intervention of Henry George – it had also emerged.

Should I call my sister and tell her, I wondered, making my way down Long Road towards the port. Tell her it's all over, time for life to take a leap forward, unstoppable as in a self-help manual, not to stand still and keep coming back, non-stop, but, in fact, to disappear. But who could say where and when it all came to a standstill. When they called me in Zagreb and told me that Daniel had gone. Or the moment I dropped the candle in the procession. Or when the war started. When Ma started stuffing herself with medicines. The first time I went into the dingo-man's Ikea apartment. Or, even – perhaps not crucial, but for me nevertheless important, the moment I suspected that Ned Montgomery had become like every other bastard who would, in the end, make a rubbish film.

There's a storm out at sea and perhaps all the houses and trees in the town will be destroyed, perhaps a real catastrophe will occur, something important and elemental, that will spin me round like a forceful slap, but not even that would shake me out of my inability to turn something round in myself, to make a quite small movement, like breathing, without collapsing. I could call her, my sister, and tell her that.

Her answer would be something I didn't want to hear, as usual. She'd say something about the fact that I shouldn't be so affected and idiotic, because life simply isn't fair, and therefore, bla bla bla, and grow up.

I hate you, sister, I thought, sometimes on Mondays, sometimes on Fridays, and sometimes all week long, but you're all I have to hold onto.

On the waterfront the south wind was destroying the palms and tamarisks, rocking the buildings and tearing out satellite dishes and air-conditioners. Tin cockerels danced on the roofs, cranes, the skeletons of mammoths, could be heard roaring above the urban skyscrapers. Their metallic roar, full of an elephantine grudge, was broken through by a feeble mouse's cry in my ear: the sudden high scream of a child that has just sustained its first injury.

Perhaps that's the same pain with which we yell out at the end.

An object, shiny and polished, a fairly serious thing, lay on the crocheted tablecloth, between the cups for milk.

'Has you been spyin' on people, Dada?'

My sister had burst through the door, upset, I could see, although she behaved quite calmly to start with. She had come late, with no make-up and her hair not done, as though someone had just hauled her out of bed. And she had thrown that box down on the table. My sister.

'Has you really been spyin' on people, Dada?'

'I haven't done anything, I just sat outside his house, on the wall.'

I hadn't done anything, really. That was the worst of it. What would she say if she knew about that whole failed sex, lies and USB mission. She'd kill me, I thought. She'd kill me even though I'd chucked the film down the drain.

She pushed the box towards me. *Something for you.*

'Oh, he told me everything – that you sits on the wall every night. Now see where it's got us. Look inside. I hope you'll calm down now. That you'll leave us all in peace – both the living and the dead,' she said.

Herr Šain had gone to her. To her, not to me, I thought.

The box he had sent her, cardboard, probably a shoe box, was stuck down round the edges.

Ma came into the kitchen like a ghost behind the green curtain, we had woken her.

'You're all we needed,' muttered my sister.

Without a word, Ma opened the top cupboard and took out sugar and coffee, lit the gas.

'This is still my house,' she said quietly.

Out of the box I took a pistol, carefully wrapped in a soft rag.

'The Colt got its name from Samuel Colt,' said the man who had sold our father the Colt as a present for Daniel. I was standing beside my father and although I'd never been interested in pistols, for an instant I coveted that Colt. The winter light gleamed on its cylinder, like an ornament. An ornamental weapon. a surprise for my brother's birthday.

Later, as he handed it to Daniel, my father said it was 'out of commission, but it had once fired very accurately'.

'D'you think this Colt ever shot anyone?' my brother asked, aiming it at me. 'Maybe it was Shane's pistol or Clyde's.'

'Don't get carried away, Daniel, it's just a broken barrel, it's not a Stradivarius,' said my sister.

A weapon isn't romantic, as someone once said, what's romantic is the death that sleeps in the barrel. As long as it just sleeps.

Samuel Colt lost two sisters and his mother while he was still a child, and his one surviving sister later committed suicide, the man who sold my father the Colt told him, I recalled. 'But he got on very well with his brothers,' he said that too.

Did all of that have anything to do with his invention? I wondered, holding the gun with the barrel pointing towards the floor.

If you try to invent a pistol, willy-nilly, you must often think about death.

Ma covered her mouth with her hand, and my sister her forehead. They looked at the object in my hands.

'Did you know that the inventor of this pistol died in poverty, although he was pretty rich most of his life?' I said, laying the object on the table. That's what the man who sold our father the pistol for Daniel told us. Death exploited and rejected Samuel Colt. But there's no doubt that he devoted his life to it.

'That's Daniel's,' said Ma.

'You just landed from Mars, Ma,' my sister snapped darkly.

She picked up the silver object for a moment, and immediately threw it down again, as though it was hot. In fact it was an unpleasantly cold piece of metal under the fingers – with a smooth wooden handle.

'That's it,' I said, collapsing onto a chair. I thrust the blue envelope that had been in the bottom of the box into my pocket, without them seeing – I felt something hard and flat in it. My heart beat a gong and stopped it between my ribs.

That's it, I repeated to myself: the answer.

The two of them studied the pistol, touched it carefully, not like a weapon, more like a sea bass that might suddenly leap off the table. They were comical.

'It's nice of the vet to give Daniel's pistol back,' said Ma.

My sister looked at me suspiciously.

Then Ma turned away from us, put the coffee pot on the heat and waited for the water to start bubbling.

C

Uncle Braco is taking us on his boat to the island. It's the only video where we're all together, apart from my father. He's filming, that's why he's not in it, but you can just occasionally hear his voice.

'The Istranka's great,' says my father, pleased with his employer's boat.

Braco, also pleased, says 'a-huh' and strokes his moustache. Ma takes beers for my father, herself and Braco out of the garish green portable fridge.

We had hung our feet into the foam and were singing: my sister and I. We were sitting on the prow and feeding each other grapes. Daniel, in striped trousers from Trieste, had climbed onto the roof of the cabin and was spitting blue skins into the sea. His spittle stuck to our hands and legs, rubbed with oil and shining in the sun.

'Yous really a savage, spitting like that,' says my sister.

'Didn't mean to.'

'So why's you spitting grapes, you clown?'

'Not my fault. The skins should be thinner,' says Daniel.

'What you say?'

The wind carries off their words and the chugging of the engine, takatakatakataka.

'The skin should be...' yells Daniel.

'Idiot,' says my sister to the camera.

'I told you he's an idiot,' she turns to me and says. 'He's spitting grapes, the skin bothers him.'

Daniel gets to his feet, his head becomes a glistening ball of sun and the adults wave at him: 'Get down, get down, you'll fall.'

Uncle Braco turns the tiller and draws back the throttle.

'A stag,' says Daniel, dancing on the roof of the cabin.

Then more loudly: 'There's a stag in the sea! People, people! There's a stag in the sea!'

'What's got into the child, inheavensname?' Uncle Braco twists round.

A wave breaks over the little Istranka at the prow and the stern; little drops spatter the screen. The sea looks plump and deeper than the sky, friable, then glassy.

The swell makes us feel sick. The dull bright light torments us.

Then the camera comes to rest and finally homes in on something that looks like a tree trunk. Our eyes try to identify something like a large brown dog.

When the boat comes closer, we can see it clearly, for a moment: the antlers, the blue belly of the corpse. One cloudy dark eye – a white tongue. The focus is suddenly lost – my father switches off the camera.

There's a herd of hoofed animals on the little island – people say that monks brought them, or that the herd belonged to Comrade Tito. People know about them, in the summer they come down to the island beach among the tourists and eat their rubbish, such as water-melon skins.

People said that in the mating season the males hear the love call of does from the mainland and swim, roaring loudly, towards the shore. Fishermen have seen sights like that in the sea: sometimes a roe-buck, and sometimes even a hungry boar in the channel.

'What d'you think happened to the doe on the shore?' Angelo asks me.

(We're sitting in my room, watching films from my box.)

'She was sad for a while,' I reply. 'And then maybe she called to a different roe-buck.'

'Evil doe.'

'Not evil, just a doe,' I say, kissing him between his imaginary antlers.

5

In a story it would say there hadn't been a wedding like it in living memory. That's what the feast at Verica Vrdovđek's was like.

Tables with white cloths stretched from the terrace of the ex-Illyria, along the waterfront on one side to the beach, and on the other to the port and pier above it. Traffic through the Settlement was stopped, holes in the asphalt repaired, streets swept, windows cleaned. Around the new statue of St Fjoko, an unusual flaming garden spread, radially, like a sound, with begonias, petunias, dazzling fuschias and dahlias, and on candelabras and over the pergolas hung pieces of real fishermen's macramé with hard knots and little geranium flowers.

It seemed as though even the air was lighter, freed of death and dust, asbestos and lead – just distilled ether, and, as in a recipe for perfume, hypnotic drifts of Lavandula angustifolia, the sweat of women's backs and tart male breath with grains of black pepper. And above it all: the fragrance of grilled meat. An electric spit turned lambs and suckling pigs and a two-month old donkey foal for the top table.

Oh yes, Vrdovđek was a prophet in his village. Torches blazed, car horns blared, bells pealed from all the little churches, flags with crowing cockerels fluttered. Onto a stage, specially made for the festivities, climbed a showbiz star with new silicon in her boobs and top lip and sang the anthem, and the Settlement rose to its light feet, with sound heart and empty belly.

'Looks like a rice pudding,' said my sister, tottering off on her twenty-centimetre heels to the bar for a caipirinha.

Does she mean the bride or the hotel? I reflected.

The bride was a scowling future matron in gilded curtains and the seventh month of pregnancy, and beside her the groom protruded, a mariolino with a thin neck and a round bleached head, which he shook in constant surprise.

The Super Mario clones had gathered up all their buckets and spades two days earlier, and behind the scaffolding a phoney palace had appeared bearing the neon sign *Villa Vrdovđek 2*.

Vrdovđek had invited everyone and was roasting lambs for the whole Settlement.

'It's not long till the election for mayor,' said my sister. 'Love goes through the stomach,' she said. Then everyone clapped the happy couple, and we joined in. It was a good show.

I recalled a local politician from Bosnia whom our friends showed us on Youtube, who had secured votes from all the bloody factions in his area and become the municipal leader, because he had a good breeding bull. We laughed and said 'would you believe it', but my sister said she could well believe it because 'that's the way things work here'. On the screen, the bull leapt onto a cow, unencumbered by prejudice.

At the table next to the host, the witnesses and the bridal couple, Maria Čarija had settled herself, the *belle du jour*, in a wedding dress cobbled together from bits of gauze and polyester. In one hand a serviette holding a piece of grilled meat, in the other a Pepsi Cola.

'Get her,' said my sister, pointing in the direction of Maria, before she staggered off for a new caipirinha. 'At least someone's got style,' she added.

Further down, near the stage, there was a stir among some of the wedding guests when on the new façade under the neon sign *a painted member*, as it would say in books, was revealed. It was a giant penetrator, a celestial howitzer, and it was cheerfully winking one eye at the astonished guests.

Some guerrilla fighter had his work cut out last night, I reflected.

Čarija did not betray any disquiet or recognition of the artistic signature, although suspicion for the devastation of the façade immediately fell on her relatives. She was entirely focused on her beauty, she passed the tips of her fingers over her forehead and the curls round her face and lowered her eyes, sucking her lips.

'Hmm, a picture speaks a thousand words,' commented my sister, grinning at the drawing. She sucked up everything under her paper umbrella fiercely. The moustached, bearded and clean-shaven glances of the men stuck to her in various currencies, I observed.

Our host quickly sorted it out. Two Super Mario clones sprang out of a van with a ladder and tin of paint and noiselessly carried out the action of sanitizing the shameless façade. Then three hefty friends of the family took hold of Čarija, as discreetly as possible, and dragged her away, *willy-nilly*.

The lusty showbiz star raised the tone once more, and two cooks moving as one bore an oval platter with a roast donkey adorned with chips and orange peel to the top table.

And everything fell into oblivion, into a shallow dish full of fat.

For a while I listened and then I heard, clearly, although from a distance, Maria's furious female scream, the old war cry of the tribe from the railway line, tapping her lips with her palm: 'Va-va-va-va...'

I was born during the reign of now forgotten technical appliances, those transitional forms that didn't survive although it seemed that their epoch would last forever. Who'd have thought something as modern and contemporary as a cassette player would so quickly and definitively end up in a museum? a video-recorder, a Walkman, a floppy disk, telephone boxes, telephone answer-machines... who still uses any of those things? In fact it's easier to find someone who plays gramophone records or someone who writes letters and sends them by post, just as there are still people who go to the cinema and film libraries. But finding someone who watches videos or has a telephone answer-machine, who walks around with a Walkman or files data on floppy disks, doesn't seem possible, ever less so, even theoretically.

'It's as though that time never existed. Everything I used to know, it's as though it's been recorded over. I just can't keep up, with that speeding-up, that bullshit, it makes you feel like a relic of the past even when you's still young,' my sister said on one occasion.

How many times in your life can you link in, I reflected. It's exhausting. In this instance, the few years between us give me an advantage after all, I concluded.

'When new things overtakes you, you thinks you's getting old, that you's been crushed by the army of the linked-in. But then again, they'll dream up something new tomorrow,' said my sister.

'Don't exaggerate, it's like keeping up with soaps, if you like – you can join in whenever,' I said.

'But still, it's an effort,' she said once – when the video-shop *Braco & Co* closed forever.

Herr Karlo Šain doesn't call back. It's pointless to call – even the answerphone doesn't respond, the telephone is off the hook.

When I shoved the blue envelope from the bottom of the box into my pocket, quickly, so that my sister and Ma wouldn't see, I had felt something flat and hard in it. But it was only later, in my room, when I took it out, that I realized it was a disk: a disk and a letter from Herr Šain.

'That's it,' I said to myself. It must be his answer.

The letter was easy, that's why it's an invention that resists, I reflected, but finding someone who saves data on a floppy disk doesn't seem possible, or someone who watches videos or has a telephone answer-machine, who walks around with a Walkman, uses a typewriter... you can't find anyone like that – ever less so, even theoretically – unless you happen to know Herr Karlo Šain. As far as gadgets are concerned, he's like those heavy metal followers in small towns who live in the nineteen-eighties. Herr Karlo is a subculture, with a membership of one.

But what can I do with his disk? I cruised through the Old Settlement decorated for the evening wedding of the decade, I cruised through the town, went into Internet Cafés and playrooms full of 'kids with fat bums' as my sister would say. But nothing. 'Computers like that are out-of-date,' said the employees of the Internet Café, smiling in a somewhat superior, somewhat one-track specialist way.

It's absolutely true that you'll get by more easily today with cuneiform script and a clay tablet than with a floppy disk in your pocket.

They say he disappeared overnight. Left. Outside his door, under the fig tree, a queue of people formed with baskets containing guinea pigs or cats or with dogs beside them, on leads.

Karlo Šain is a dark avatar who suddenly vanishes then reappears. Who leaves questions and answers. Who opens his jaws and says, unexpectedly sadly and pleasantly: 'I don't ask anything of life, other than a little radiance.'

I asked my sister whether she thought he was in some way a fool of God. a fool of God, like Prince Mishkin, Arturo Bandini or Alan Ford. Like Tim Burton's characters played by Johnny Depp, and sometimes Helena Bonham-Carter, only bigger and uglier. Young Hamsun, pure and hungry in the crystal cold of Kristiania, until he became a Nazi, I reflected. Amadeus, Van Gogh... Anaïs Nin, for sure.

'My dear, the only fools of God I knows are you and Calimero,' said my sister, in a slightly mocking way. 'And Warhol,' she then added, more seriously, after a brief reflection.

That gilt, that radiance, how does he see it? I imagine it as two cappuccinos in St Mark's Square in Venice, Christmas in Vienna, white tablecloths and china for breakfast under a cloudless sky, a red sports car with a young woman in it, whom we watch from the beach (she's wearing a silk dress that you could fold to fit into your hand). Or German poetry in leather binding that someone's neighbour with clear eyes reads on her balcony right beside the sea. Now, in September, the radiance is in Dubrovnik. In a gallery or concert hall, radiance is discreet. It gleams on the sides of cruisers as they sail out of the western harbour at night under lights, *Oasis of the Seas, Crystal Serenity, MSC Splendida*: music on the deck and a mini-theatre under the prow. Radiance is in the varnish and in the way in which the willowy waiter serves a dessert of bitter chocolate and chillies in a Tuscan cafeteria, while in winter radiance beams down on a skating rink on top of a Russian fur hat. That's how I imagine it, never having travelled anywhere.

It may be that radiance is a confection, the cold glamour of the moon, false or petty-bourgeois like operetta, painting or those receptions after exhibition openings. I really don't know whether it can be entered into, whether radiance has three dimensions or not a single one, but the thought of it is always brilliant and lively and round like that magic lantern.

Radiance is best noticed, Herr Šain, where it's been and gone or when it's observed from that dark place where it's never been. That's the first thing I discovered in connection with it. Go on, just take a look at the complete absence of radiance we have here, a matt night full to the brim with darkness.

If I don't ride, I walk; the key thing is not to stop in one place too long. Sometimes I run as well. When I first moved to Zagreb, I fancied a man who lived in the Trnje district, so I often ran to him, from the student hostel to Trnje, a place of tribulation. Through tribulation to the stars was already a well-worn route, but not for me. To start with I ran because I was too impatient to see him to wait for the tram, I recall. Once the clasp on my sandal broke, so I ran barefoot. Who knows what my PE teacher would have said – at school I didn't like running, I used to get out of it.

I believed I was in love with the man from Trnje. But there are limits to your stamina for running towards someone who doesn't run towards you. And one day I turned back several streets before his house and ran off in the opposite direction. Afterwards I couldn't remember anything especially important or especially nice in connection with that man, apart from the running. It must actually have been the running I fell for rather than him.

In the dawn following Vera Vrdovđek's feast, I found myself for the first time in ages once again speeding through the streets. As other people might lose a child, I had lost Ma. To start with I walked around looking for her, then I began to call her. The Settlement was empty, beer bottles and single use plastic cups rolled through the un-swept lanes, while cats fought over pieces of roast meat left under the tables, scattering bones over the asphalt.

At the Little Lagoon, I caught sight of one of Mother's shoes, under a bench. I picked it up and set off at a run. I ran down Long Road then across the street and there in the window of one of the houses I saw Žana Mateljan, a girl who had once lived in our neighbourhood.

'Is everything OK with your mum?' called Žana looking at the shoe in my hand. 'She was here this morning, she rang the doorbell around five in the morning and asked whether some old married couple live here.'

'And?'

'And?! I told her no, we were a young married couple, we got married in April, and I looked down at the ground, because I was embarrassed. Your mother has known me from birth, after all.'

'And?'

'And?! And then she asked me why I was looking at her shoes, did I mean that they needed polishing. Her shoes. I wasn't looking at her shoes at all, but at the ground. And I wasn't thinking anything. I told her I thought her footwear was perfectly fine and didn't need polishing.'

'She read the name on the door,' I said. On the door, it said *Mateljan*. 'And?'

'And she thought, for some reason, that her friend Mariana lived here with her husband, she got lost,' I said.

'Well, there you are, your Mum announced that she knew what I was thinking about: she said I must've been thinking that I'd give her shoes a good brushing. Then she thanked me and went off towards the highway. And I don't give a toss about her shoes, I mind my own business,' said Žana Mateljan.

I ran along the stream, over the highway, as far as the railway and beyond, to the viaduct and then back, with the shoe in my hand the whole time.

Ma didn't come home last night. It wasn't until early in the morning, when I was woken by thirst, that I noticed she wasn't in her bed or anywhere else in the whole house. If I run I don't think, if I don't think, I can run and run like this for hours and then stumble on her, but if I stop, maybe I'll never be able to get going again, I reflected.

I found her on the slipway. She was awake and appeared uninjured. I gave her the shoe and she put it on without a word.

'Here, Cinderella,' I said. Then I called an ambulance.

'You's really going,' says my sister.

'I'm really going,' I say and carry on chopping onion and meat for lunch.

Ma's in hospital. My sister is driving me to the station. The afternoon train to Zagreb, then 'Berlin via München' I'd said. 'Then I'll see,' I said. My room-mate is waiting for me there for us to make tortillas together, for our legs to swell up with standing and the stench of paprika, onion and oil to get under our fingernails, but maybe – when we emerge into the street, stepping out loudly, our boots' heels beating out a harmonized rhythm – maybe a city, infinite as the world, will spread out around us, one of the centres of the universe, which we wouldn't be able to cross in a hundred days. Maybe all the restaurants and clubs keep going till morning, maybe their doors will fly open like at airports and we'll go in, carefree as girls in a film; inside everywhere is warm, light and spacious, and maybe I'll forget what I'm leaving, my own self, this ass-hole of the world. 'Your young hair will turn grey, but your grey heart will be made young,' said some poet we read at school.

'It's a bit helter-skelter, this Berlin thing of yours. You decides things too fast, it's because you's still green and juvenile,' said my sister.

'It's temporary,' I said.

'Of course it's temporary. I only hope it's got nothing to do with the box and the pistol?'

'I'm all done with the box, you know that,' I lie brazenly, not wanting to talk about it any more.

My sister must never know about the correspondence on the floppy disk. Neither she nor Ma – as long as we're alive. Especially now Ma has ended up in hospital, I reflected. All they need now would be Daniel's cyber-postal fairy tale with his fat friend.

When they ask if I'm OK, they expect me to tell them I'm OK, I sense. I expect the same thing from them, for that matter. That they should be OK, or at least not to be in a bad way, or at least not to tell me.

My suitcase is waiting beside the table in the kitchen in which nothing has changed since my birth, and perhaps not even since my sister's. The Obodin fridge and red top-cupboard, grease in the gaps between the ceramic tiles and the gas canister with newspapers piled on it. Through the window, always the same view with the changing seasons and rare feastdays. On Long Road there are still little flags flapping, left over from Verica Vrdovđek's feast.

Maybe there'll be no Old Settlement soon, I reflected.

The *Illyria* hotel was mine more than it could ever be Vrdovđek's, but still there's absolutely nothing I can do about the fact that it has vanished, I reflected. I can go and draw a cock on it, that's all. And they'll paint over it and that'll be that. 'The wolf ate the ass,' *the insatiable one* would say.

'You don't feed yourselves properly,' said my sister. Of Ma and me. 'And you're both good cooks, former and future.' She was winding us up.

I don't know what's bad about goulash. 'I'm cooking this for Ma, I promised. She has a problem with vegetarian dishes. She says, if there's no meat or fish, I don't get what's the main thing on the plate and what goes with what,' I said and went on cutting up the pieces of meat. The onion was sizzling in the oil and smelling good.

'What an approach to food, hierarchical! Patriarchal, in essence,' said my sister. 'You's bleedin',' she said. My finger was stinging, but the knife was sharp, so I hadn't felt the blade. I thought the blood came from the animal.

'That knife is ruddy,' she said, tossing it into the sink. She took my hand and sucked the blood out of my finger, then spat into the sink as well. And twice more. Fingers always bleed inordinately, I reflected.

'You taste of iron, ruddy-Rusty,' she said, spitting. She hadn't called me that in ages. She washed my hand with alcohol and bound it tightly with a cloth. Then she wiped her lips, carefully dabbing them, not to spoil her lipstick.

'Ma's goin' to come to my place when she gets out of hospital, and we'll let or sell the house,' said my sister.

OK. I don't care any more. Let them sell the house. I watched the blood seeping through the cloth. 'OK,' I said.

My sister tossed the meat into the pan, then sat down opposite me, laid her hands in her lap, sighed, and looked at me as at a lost cause.

She sat down opposite me, laid her hands in her lap and crossed her legs, with her feet in little sandals with high pointy heels. Those sandals were attached to her feet only by two tiny straps, one round her ankle, and the other over her toes, I observed. She moved about in shoes like that as freely as it was possible to do, sometimes even running down steps like a chamois down a mountain. The high heels demanded concentration on one's feet, watchfulness, as when you're in charge of a vehicle, I reflected. Even in a woman like my sister who wore them every day.

She saw I was watching her.

'High heels is a weapon,' she said displaying her pedicured foot.

'An objectively lovely foot in a lovely sandal,' her former husband had once said and I recalled that as well. But she still left him, I reflected.

In recent years my sister had grown rounder and heavier like some mythic woman. 'A Valkyrie,' Herr Professor said of her. 'There is no hero here to measure his strength against such a Valkyrie,' he said. He's right, I thought, it's rotten luck, beside her men seemed either weak or coarse.

She lost the sharpness of her elbows and knees, acquired fleshy thighs and forearms, but she retained her slender joints, suppleness in her hips and the head of a little girl. Like that woman from the print in the toilet of the *Last Chance* under which is written P. P. Reubens: 'Venus Frigida'.

But when she appears on those heels, I can easily imagine her also with a tail, like that English lady holding a glass of champagne, putting on make-up and at the same time – thanks to her tail – smoking.

'I think Marilyn Monroe was wrong about high heels and women's insecurity,' said my sister suddenly, seriously and as though addressing her shoes. 'High heels is shoes for the brave.'

Marilyn had said, roughly, that women who wore high heels were attractive because they looked insecure. Marilyn was just flirting when she made that announcement, I thought. Just as she was flirting with her insecurity, I thought.

'What kind of world is it where Marilyn Monroe has issues of self-confidence,' said my sister. 'What hope is there for the rest of us?'

I shrugged my shoulders: I don't want to think about my feet while I walk the way women in high heels must. I want just to walk, and not to be aware of my shoes. I'd rather take off my T-shirt and go around naked on a hot day than put on heels like that, there'd certainly be more freedom in that kind of courage, and more sense. That's roughly what I said to her.

Then I added that Marilyn Monroe had proved that flirting could kill you if you made it too much of a habit. Like Kurt Cobain too, for that matter. Death was part of their performance. Mayakovsky, Yesenin and Isadora Duncan plus their fans, that whole Russian chain gang, focused on themselves. I said that, roughly.

I think it saddened her, I wasn't expecting that.

'I don't like it when you talks like that,' she said drily, although I'd never talked like that to her before.

She was just happy because of her new shoes.

It isn't pure fetishism, I reflected. High heels are part of her, a continuation. What do I know about her freedom?! When she's wearing slippers she really does look disarmed.

What do I know about her courage, she's the one who's staying, I thought, watching my sister walking in front of me as she crosses the hospital linoleum as though it was a red carpet, towards the exit. She's carrying a plastic bag and an empty Tupperware box, which had contained goulash and macaroni, as though it was a new handbag. She is that radiance Herr Karlo talked about, all waiting rooms have revolting air and are colourless. 'That girl's luxury,' her former husband would have said and he'd grin, but much good did it do him.

Perfume–hair–footsteps.

Hospital–goulash–Mother.

'When you open the door of a hospital, you open a Pandora's box,' said one of the several great-aunts who used to visit *the insatiable one* in the years of her illness, nodding their hairdos, but I don't remember which of those old ladies it was. They would pat me on the top of my head and stick crisps in my mouth, as in a mini communion. The three of us didn't particularly interest them because we were the poor relations' children, a pain in the ass. One of them asked Ma if she had a lover, I recall that. And when Ma replied, embarrassed, that she hadn't, the great-aunt said: 'Ah, my dear, we'll never make a lady of you.'

Let's go out into the sun, I thought. Onto the surface. The air here is desperate.

As a child I'd been afraid of getting lost down below, in the hospital basement, among the loonies. Now, I was equally nauseated on all the floors.

'This is the only ward where we're allowed to smoke,' said Ma as we swung up and down the corridor where three skinny women in nightdresses were smoking.

I recalled Millimetre, the lunatic who used to appear in the Settlement every few years, walking ceaselessly and counting the metres and holding at least one cigarette in different stages of being smoked in each hand. His figure embodied my need for walking and Mother's dependence on smokes like a mirror image. I said that to Ma and she shook her head. I wasn't able to interpret that gesture.

'The doctor says I'll be going home on Friday,' she says.

'Super,' says my sister. 'They must be full up for the weekend.'

Ma ate the goulash – and all the macaroni, and then mopped up the sauce with bread and then we had to leave 'so as not to miss the train,' said my sister.

'Off you go,' said Ma. When I looked back from the exit, she was already in bed, with her back to the door.

People who have been lucky sometimes talk about the worst and best days or the worst and best nights of their life. We who have been less lucky don't talk about that, we know there are days after which things can be good or bad, but nothing can any longer be the worst or the best.

During the night Ma went missing, I finally managed to open the floppy disk. And that was the end of my quest. Get your stuff together it's time to leave, I reflected. *All you could have done, you've done well, take the money and run.*

Say farewell to the house, it's going under the hammer, to the cowboys on the wall who someone else will soon tear down – farewell, guys, you were true, and to ginger Jill – 'bye. And farewell to Angelo as well. He's expecting me today, at six. The train pulls out at four. At six-fifteen Angelo will call for the first time, at seven he'll come to my house. He'll wait till eight, out of sight, and then he'll start to feel stupid and he'll be angry. At ten he'll be worried. Tomorrow he'll find out that I've left. In a week he'll go back to the woman in the sports car, or someone else. He'll puff on his harmonica to blow out the dust and start playing.

In a hundred days I'll get over it, in a thousand days I'll forget.

That's not the worst or the best story in my life.

Dear Dada,

Plucky girl! Forgive me for not having returned the letter you left on the garden table when you visited me, the letter I sent four years ago from Perm to your brother. I've decided to keep it as a memento. (It's strange that when we lose those dear to us, we constantly seek proof from ourselves that we loved them enough. And, have you noticed, no proof is enough.)

I'm sending you back the spotted salamander, however, maybe you'll have somewhere to stick it.

For a long time, I thought that it's best to leave the dead to sleep, let the living rest in peace—as though that were possible. In the end, I came back here for the same reason you did. But, I don't know whether you've found your truth, I myself have certainly not found peace. If it exists anywhere, it is not in the Old Settlement for me. I needed to come back, to travel a long road, to come back to some sort of beginning, nothing, zero, to where I am now. But where to now? Movement, some people find their home in wandering, you understand that.

I'm sending via your sister what I should have given you long ago (cowardice created mediation, the guilt of the go-between), Daniel's old Colt and some of his written words, topsy-turvy, I should mention, pasted onto this floppy disk. You'll notice his touching effort—to be like everyone else. What chance of that is there for a poet, or a revolutionary, a cosmologist, a red-haired child, and an over-educated fat vet in a town without metaphysics?

In the morning we slaughter a pig, in the afternoon we contemplate Hölderlin, such is life.

I won't go on, those are things that have followed me through the years, through the metropolises and never-never lands of this everywhere volatile, jaded world.

These notes belong to you, most of all. As the wise poet Cavafy said of the beloved voices of those who have died: '... sometimes in one's thoughts the mind hears them. And

for an instant through their sound the sounds of the first
song of our life come back—like music fading out in a distant
night.' That sound, the colour of a voice and its rhythm
are forever inscribed in private letters, and with them also
a look, a breath, a movement such as scratching the nose,
rubbing the brow, a familiar finger hurriedly searching for
the right letter for the right words on a keyboard.

With warmest wishes, till we meet again, somewhere,

your Friend

Daniel's letters

Subject: about bloody time ☺
From: blondie@smail.com
To: ksain@veterinarski.hr

Hey Prof! I had a helluva time googling your address on the damn pages of the vets association id never heard of before. if im in luck and luck is something im proverbially out of maybe youll find this one day. problem is the following, you scarpered and you've not been here nearly three months now and I never had a chance to explain what happened, all ill say is im sorry and you get in touch. write! write! write! cheers Daniel you know who

Subject: incident
From: blondie@smail.com
To: ksain@veterinarski.hr

Hey Prof! this is getting like Mulder and Scully. dont know if you got my earlier mail and if this address for beasties functions at all or if its just a trick for form's sake. havent the faintest what town and state youre in now, man, no one knows if youve fallen off the planet or what the hell. joking apart tho' I hope you've recovered and that you're alive and well and I want to thank you in connection with the incident that you haven't turned anyone in I know it happened because of me. anyway, I was an idiot to give them the key of your house but I want to tell you one thing, on my honour, I thought it wd all just be a joke. I didnt think it through but you have to believe me or I don't know what I'll do.

They told me Daniel either you're sucking the prof's dick or give us the key, roughly. and that there's a film of you abusing a guy but no ones seen it just everyones talking.

And then I gave them the key, what could I do. they promised they wouldnt touch you or the animals just give you a bit of a jolt cos you deserve it they said. cos you lure boys ☹.

got to go now my bus for school is coming and my bikes bust again cos the devil always craps on a pile and a bird never craps on me. the worst is tiny the one with the low brow and goat's beard keeps saying he'll do me in when he sees me. aha but im not afraid of him or any of those sons of bitches. as if. only when I think of those poor animals they killed I feel like crying and you and everything I want to take my pistol thats still at your place and take out the whole gang fuck me if I wouldn't cos I would. rushing now d.

Subject: deep trouble ☹
From: blondie@smail.com
To: ksain@veterinarski.hr

   hey old mate karlo where are you? its two months since my first email. I beg you in Gods name to get in touch so I know your alive and arent mad and after that whatever. in any case ill keep writing every day whats new not that anyone talks to me anymore. weve fallen out as you can imagine cos theyre afraid ill talk and now theyre blackmailing me as well. cos i'm not going back to them. at home its the same old social welfare mournful grey brown with black tones. now its winter and slimy and wet and mud, indescribable gloom. someone says sea but who sees the sea your not a crazy tourist you feel even sadder when it stretches out in front of you like a blue whale. I go to the caff to play poker only in the settlement is there still poker. everyone smokes weed and spends the whole afternoon spaced then they screw some chick and come back in a year's time and smoke weed. I think since the tedious war ended and already a whole cockful of time has passed everyone wherever you go is chewing over the same tedious stories that have fuck all to do with me I was born too late even for the pioneers apart from the idea that my damn tedious life is passing in this fucking ass-hole of a place. its only on the screen that I see real life. not a word from Rusty who knows what film shes in now at uni in zg, shes probably run into some fucker again whos wound her up and now shes fantasizing about eternal love and that rot. she was a bit cleverer when she fought guys he he. but at least if she was here. I dont see the older one which is faaar better you understand what a snake she is he he. and ma like ma comes home from work done in and has a bit of a tipple. horror story.

lately ive been like an owl to tell you the truth. its not advisable to hang out with me everyones shit-scared of the gang. only tomi iroquois sometimes greets me in the street but he isnt really friends with me any more either hes probably afraid of getting a bollocking from the sons of bitches. and theres no point anyone else getting screwed because of me. for the rest theres a funny little chick I fancy that could be the only good news lets say altho you never know with these love things whether its good or bad. the downside is shes ears sister and hes now the big cheese and theres always a kid around with a harmonica we always used to burn his pens but now hes come back from america strutting his stuff. school so-so. got 'a' for croatian. d.

Subject: RIP gecko
From: blondie@smail.com
To: ksain@veterinarski.hr

salute! me again! thought of you today when ma killed a gecko that lived on the terrace and that you called by a name I thought was a kind of iced cake. in winter it hid in our corridor and now it's snuffed it. how stupid how can people think that such a useful creature is poisonous I cant believe it including that mother of mine. how can it be dangerous when the creature is transparent you can virtually see its inner organs. if youre wondering about jill I havent mentioned her shes well like a cat she eats sleeps purrs walks on roofs. im fucked. otherwise I like February there are those few days of false spring and when I get out of the morning shift I have two or three hours to get down to the beach. only you cant go down even to the little lagoon any more without running into those sons of bitches my former friends. friends indeed. that little ear the younger barić got banged up too and sometimes that Angelo angel eyes I mentioned to you that came back from america and plays the harmonica and some other types from the centre. not tomi iroquois his dad got him a job on the railway and he slaves and hell soon have to get married cos hes got sanjica in the family way. married for gods sake and not yet eighteen. and the tiny shithead has got himself a pitbull that he leads on a rope without a muzzle. their latest game is putting the screws on kids behind the tech. I heard from dada she isnt coming I really miss her altho in recent years shes thought she was something else hey im only kidding. I know shes always Rusty at heart. that girl I told you I fancy shes got measles so shes staying home its stupid to have measles when youre not a kid. regardless of everything ive written to you things are sometimes so bad for me I cant describe its like someone gouged out my stomach. incidentally did you know that ned montgomery nearly died form the aftermath of measles some years ago thats really bizarre at the end after all hes almost a super hero. you fix all the bad guys and sons of bitches and then youre fucked by some measles amoeba.

   daniel if you remotely remember

Subject: animal stuff
From: blondie@smail.com
To: ksain@veterinarski.hr

   today there was a programme on national geographic about chameleons. you remember the spotted chameleon was the only little picture of the animal kingdom that absolutely no one in the old settlement had when we were kids they must not have made enough pictures. maybe youll be amused to know that somewhere in a drawer I still have an album and an empty place for that forgotten ace of a spotted chameleon. imagine remembering that.

Subject: hospital
From: blondie@smail.com
To: ksain@veterinarski.hr

   ah well now I realize youre never going to get these emails and that the address is crap but there. today I spent a bit of time in hospital cos I got involved in a row and got two stitches in the temple. the first and only time till this morning id been there since my old man died. the point is that dada and I knew hed had it and wouldnt be coming back but we shoved that all away in ourselves and pretended it was nothing for as long as we could and we were ok until we got to the stinking hospital. in intensive care I saw that srećko type who was in the bed next to our old man. all bandaged up like a mummy cos he had shot himself in the mouth and blown his face off. the whole façade. a nurse was standing by his bed trying to get him to respond srećko srećko wake up come on you have to stay awake. imagine the fucking mess. when I cried everyone thought it was cos my old man had died but I wasnt thinking of my dead dad at all I was just crying cos I was afraid and thinking of that srećko who had such shitty luck he survived and is now a million times more fucked.

'bye your friend d.

Subject: cosmos
From: blondie@smail.com
To: ksain@veterinarski.hr

im not doing anything just rotting at home and watching documentaries on national geographic. I dont like looking at earthquakes and floods tidal waves and such catastrophic crap. some say what the hell thats all people deserve when theyre so arrogant it puts them in their place. as tho they werent people fuck it all as tho they were some superior folk who dont squirt spray into the ozone or as tho they were hypermoral types. and in the end its always the poorest who get the roughest deal in these tornadoes and typhoons and earthquakes theres no justice. theres only justice in films. is nature just? no way. are people? like hell. thats why I like films about space best where theres no nature or society. if I cd measure the stars like tycho brahe id like that. you think everything up there is dead if it isnt alive. space is hyperactive all those black holes meteorites protuberances like rings and with tails. and fusions of hydrogen with helium helium with hydrogen. fusions in the great belly of arcturus the brightest of all the stars with a gigantic yolk that those who are here next spring will see. and the pulsar the pulse of space the lighthouse of space that beats kaboom kaboom like a heart, comes into being after a supernova explodes and rotates very fast. imagine a space lighthouse a galactic rotor. id really like to see that. or neptune's sea of diamonds. be a person who looks closely at the stars an astronomer a stargazer ptolomey and nikolaus copernicus or that lyudmila karachkina you told me about who named all her asteroids after artists so that in the sky there is a charlie chaplin star and a planet dostoevksy. if you cant be an astronaut be an astronomer and so what if you cant walk on other stars discover one fall in love with it give it a name. the stars gave a name to someone called tycho brahe how could he possibly have chosen another profession with a name like that I wonder. its not like that fancy boulevard of the stars in Hollywood celebrities and the like. my stars would be like sheriffs badges and partisan stars in constellations the only people who cd get them wd be a true person if he was brave and good. high wide deep. in the galaxies there wont be the twinkling names of thieves murderers and criminals whove made themselves filthy bloody millions which are badges on earth because they just thought how to make money and left us without any beauty. the president of space will never honour them. let them be given shitty streets in their pathetic states where people die of alcohol hunger violence neglect. who gives a fuck about people. or those conformist pests who sell their souls and betray people for small change. and the constellations wont have the names of those sods who shat on love and friendship cowards who at the key moment crawl off into their holes. in a word there wont be either big or small sons of bitches in the solar systems just old verified gods, gauchos and the true cowboys among us great lads and lasses will get the radiant badge of space.

d.

Western

WHATEVER HAPPENED TO THE HEROES? WHATEVER HAPPENED TO THE HEROES?

THE STRANGLERS

In a black and white film, a serious-looking guy says in a fatherly tone: *'Go west, young man. There you will find wealth, fame and adventure.'*

The time of day, the weather, the town and the room, nothing is specified – it resembles all the places he's been and the times he was there, all at once. He feels warmth, a pulsing in his groins, happiness round the corner, barely supportable but unstoppable, and that's how he knows he's young and strong, and the sky is bright in the town, or maybe it's on an island – because he can hear the sea and the sound of a moped. Some rays of sunlight penetrate through the curtain on the balcony, flicker in the open doorway, over the shoulders and naked thigh of his wife and shine on her brown mane. She is sleeping. He presses his lips into her back. He enters her without waking her, slowly and deeply, seeking in that depth the mystery far inside a woman, which overwhelms him every time. He holds her in his arms, and his mouth is full of her hair. He draws her to him with a hint of fear from backstage that this is all going to stop. These are the first years of our marriage, he thinks, and he lays his hand against her bare belly, chews her hair, her nape. As he presses himself against her backside, through the open balcony he sees this same wife of his crossing the road in a white raincoat and a Ferrari suddenly speeding up, knocking her down and running over her, over her head, and then in reverse, back over her bird-like ribs. His wife becomes a plastic blow-up doll with round lips for rubber cunnilingus, and the Ferrari's vermillion tempera disperses, flooding the image, the balcony, filling the room, the bed, his mouth, his nose and the television set.

Before his eyes fill completely with blood, Ned catches sight of a man on the television in a black and white fatherly voice repeating: *'Go west, young man. There you will find wealth, fame and adventure.'* And now the adverts.

Go west, young man. And there you will find wealth, fame and adventure.

Holy shit, turn it down!

Go west, young man and there you will find/ Go west, young man and there you will find/ Go west, young man...

'Hey, you! Hey, kid! Hey, Tod, damn your eyes! Someone's trying to sleep here, for God's sake! Turn that bloody thing off!'

He tries to say that, he hears the words in his head, but his tongue won't obey him, it lies in the bottom of his mouth, like something dead.

'Well, well – Ned, you're alive. You've forgotten what today is? It's half past two, man, we've not got much daylight left. We have to show up at the shoot, man, it'd be OK to get there on time, you know,' says Tod. 'At least for the final showdown.'

Ned tries to raise his head, but it doesn't work, it's nailed to the pillow.

'You recognized that, eh? Who says: go west, young man? Senator, it's Senator, what's his name... Sorry, I'll be right back, that's my mobile,' says Tod.

'And why the fucking fuck, go fucking west. What a damn idiotic fascination. Myth. Any shithead with any brains and a few dollars in his pocket goes to the bloody east these days. Near, far, and the not-so-far east – whatever. Why even such a mega shit as me goes east,' replies Ned Montgomery, but his words still refuse to emerge from him.

After a few tottering false starts, he gets up, straightens and staggers towards the toilet.

'What a dream, oh my God, what a bloody nightmare,' he thinks. 'When I drink, I always dream the same crap.'

When Tod had tipped him onto the bed early that morning, drunk and filthy from the previous night, he had pulled off his trousers and soiled underpants – they were tossed down behind a chair – and now Ned, at this moment, leaning against the wall, notices his thin hairy legs, knobbly knees and drooping balls a little surprised, as though he is seeing that jumble of skin, hair and organs for the first time.

Tod is sitting at the improvized desk where there is a laptop, a few unwashed coffee cups and a scatter of Snickers wrappers. He is smoking a cigar.

'When we get to the final showdown, did you know, man, that in *Gunfight at OK Corral* 34 bullets were fired in five minutes. But it took them four days to shoot those five minutes! You didn't know? What kind of film star are you, man?!' he shouts to Ned through the half-open toilet door.

What in hell's name is that dickhead Tod doing now?

Ned tries to aim at the toilet bowl, but his urine trickles in a feeble, painful stream down his legs onto the tiles. He curses, wipes himself down with toilet paper and flushes the cistern, leaning his full weight on the handle.

Tod is now sitting on the floor of their apartment, with three remotes in front of him, clicking on a laptop with one hand and holding a mobile under his chin.

'Look!' he whispers in Ned's direction, gesturing towards the new film on the television.

John Wayne really was a tall son of a bitch, taller than me, Ned thinks, squinting at the TV and swaying towards the mini-bar. Since he quit smoking, he has needed increasing quantities of whisky and beer.

In front of Tod there is a large cardboard box crammed with videocassettes. a black video player, dating from the late nineteen-eighties, is farting and purring.

'What the...'

Tod tosses him a pair of his underpants from the pile of clean clothes that the maid brought that morning washed and ironed: 'Put those on, man, you look spectral; skin and bone. Your damned tool is fatter than your leg.'

'... hell is that?' Ned finishes his sentence, trying to squeeze the whisky from the bottom of the bottle into a glass.

'These?! Westerns. Recorded from the tele, hey, hey. Oh you wouldn't believe it. I've been looking at them all morning, my bro. I'm crammed with noble emotions, man. Look me in the eye! I feel somehow mythic. At least until I look at you. Sweet Jesus, Ned, you've become a carcass. a phantom. You're destroying my ideals, man.'

Ned finally pulls on his underpants, flops into an armchair and yawns broadly.

Wayne known as Courage, drunk, fires at a rat and says to the ugly girl: 'You can't take out an injunction on a rat, you gotta either let it go or kill it.'

An optimistic approach, thinks Ned. That's why the damned idealism of westerns kicked the fucking bucket. Time trampled them.

'You have to learn to live like a rat, Johnny,' says Ned to the TV.

'A girl brought us this box, full of cassettes, this morning. a devotee of yours, man, you know those dolls,' Tod goes on. 'She wants Mr Montgomery to have it – why, imagine. I said, go on, honey, don't worry give it to Uncle Tod. And I took her by her little hand. He, he. a doll, get it?! When she went out the door, I thought the box would be going straight in the trash, but in the end, you see, I've had a good time with these films, man. Like I was a bloody child again, d'you get.'

'Chuck it in the damned trash, what'll I do with it.'

Those fans are sick, they keep bringing him all kinds of bloody rubbish. Can you actually be a fan and at the same time be a normal man or, specially impossible, a normal woman, thinks Ned.

'Hey, Ned, look, there are some of your films as well. 'Virgil's Return."

'Chuck that shit in the trash and let's go to the damned shoot.'

Before leaving, he takes a look in the mirror and tries to pull his stomach in. In the end he gives up and simply takes his shirt out of his jeans. Tod's right, he looks like an old fart, he thinks.

'Well, sister, the time has come for me to ride hard and fast,' Wayne's voice can be heard as they close the apartment door.

It's going to be a bad day even for people with less luck.

Everything points to it, Ned, it would've been better if you'd stayed in bed.

'You coming, man?' Tod yells from the lift.

'Let's go, sister, the time has come for us to ride hard and fast,' replies Ned, pressing the 0 button.

It's a sunny day in Majurina. Čarija and Tomi's three triplets stand on different sides of a wire fence, talking.

'Pa says 'e'll frash yous if yous mentions the dead again,' says one of the little blond girls.

Maria looks at them longingly: Tomi's triplets won't let her hug them or pick them up. She'd carry them to and fro, up the field and down the field, until they grew big, she'd dress them in party skirts. She'd sing to them. Since she first heard them crying in the next-door house, here in Majurina, she thinks only of them. She thinks of her hens as well, because they're her responsibility.

'Pssst, listen, the dead occupiers is clattering their little bones under the earth,' says Maria Čarija.

''s not true,' says one of the triplets. 'Tomi says you's barmy.'

Maria offers them rubber sweets through the wire fence.

'Here, signorinas – and ask your teacher! All the pits and streams is full of the bones of the dead occupiers,' says Maria.

'But we doesn't go to school, Aunty Maria, we's too little. You's talking rot.'

'Anyone can see you don't go to school! Eating sweets with filthy hands,' says Maria, spitting on her skirt and using it to clean her nieces' little fingers as they push them through the fence.

Later, Maria Čarija puts on her patent-leather boots, pink, a bit scuffed, with broken heels, and thrusts her things into a plastic bag: a comb, dry twigs, a Rubik cube, lip salve and hair slides. And since she feels that the bag is half-empty, she adds what is to hand: one of her father's socks, a route map of Croatia, mascara, two used pairs of panties with lace, *L'Italiano per Lei*, and a pebble she found by the railway line. Satisfied and quite ready, she sets out to look for her hen.

This keeps happening: she finds the hen, with white feathers, a whole kilometre beyond Majurina, where the cowboys are making their film.

Maria calls to the hen: 'Come chook, come chook, chook-chook-chook.'

That call is familiar to starlings and pheasants, they all come for the grain, all except that one hen.

Around the container trucks and tents down on the flatland, a small garden has sprung up with a wooden fence and a mini-chicken coop. They've brought in feathered extras and they feed them with GM maize, which Čarija's hen is mad about and goes charging off against the natural limitations of her kind: showing distinct signs of curiosity and free will.

In some poultry sense, she is the first astronaut to have descended from the Milky Way.

★

At the filling station, Ned Montgomery watches his agent Tod pour petrol in a short-sleeved T-shirt bearing the inscription Big Black. Tod's smooth, bald head gleams in the sun, his big blue eyes squint in the sun, and his big feminine backside sways after him, as though it has a life apart from the rest of his body. All in all, if it weren't for his beard, Tod would look like a fat woman, thinks Ned.

Tod pays and comes back with a heap of Snickers for himself and two cans of beer for his passenger. It suddenly occurs to Ned, clutching the steering wheel in an effort to control the way his hands are shaking, like a disagreeable discovery his own organism had hidden from him, like, for instance, a wart in a private place, that this damned son of a bitch Tod is the only person in the world on whom, at this moment, he can rely, the only one, since his wife died, who takes some kind of care of him.

How did it happen that Ned Montgomery has become the more fucked-up half of the Ned and Tod team?! Thinks Ned.

They look like those pairs of comics, dancers or gay designers. But it could be worse, damn it all; they could be Ned and Ted.

He doesn't remember which came first, Chiara's death or bank-ruptcy and mortgage or divorce and all that bloody chaos that crashed down onto him while he was sleeping, blind drunk and totally stoned, on the floor of some hotel room.

But if your name is Ned Montgomery, some bastard named Tod will usually show up to put you under the shower and settle your bills. That's a piece of luck, probably.

However you look at it, I am at the tender mercies of my fucking agent Tod, this bloody freak who wears T-shirts with the names of damn bands, smokes stinking cigarettes like bloody Orson and who I didn't even know till four years ago, thinks Ned. I don't even know if I like or loathe him.

But anyway there's nothing to be done right now, drink up your beer, put yourself in the hands of Jesus and be grateful, Montgomery.

A little girl with peroxide hair had washed and polished the pick-up's windows: in the windscreen is clear bright sky, motionless and aseptic blue, evidence that perfection exists. a few moments before a real autumnal northerly gale had got up, shaving the town and Old Settlement dry.

'Oh man, that's some evil wind, let's go,' he says, banging the car door, climbing into the passenger seat and lighting a cigarette, that damn brute, his co-producer, co-screen-writer, co-pilot, co-friend, Tod.

At the same time:

Down on the exposed flatland, among the burrs, in front of the pre-fab town, the cameraman, the director, assistants and the whole retinue of actors are swallowing dust, smoking and staring into the distance waiting for Montgomery's pick-up.

The old man has let them know he's not satisfied with the scenes of the final showdown. They'll have to shoot them again, he said. In his damn presence, he said. He hadn't seemed all that interested in the film, he hadn't appeared all this time, so why does he suddenly care about the final showdown? The film crew wonders.

Some gunslinger extras from the local gun club are sitting on a little wall beside the chicken-coop behind the horse paddock, some distance from the rest of the team. They're on their way back from a shooting contest. Some of them have spent the morning trickling spit and making little muddy oases between their feet, others loading their weapons for practice. They keep together, but apart from the rest of the team, drinking beer and saying nothing. Waiting makes them nervous.

One of them has taken his weapon out of the club's minivan and is shooting at empty bottles; the others join him readily. They have shattered the bottles into tiny pieces and shifted their aim to the hens, which, not suspecting anything bad, are calmly pecking a few metres away and just occasionally squawking, disturbed by the splintering glass.

The lads are trying to shoot their heads off with one shot, and for the time being it's going well.

The hens don't even get a chance to spread their wings in surprise and squawk, before a bullet whines and guillotines them. Some run around headless, others fall at once, as though scythed.

'Idleness is evil, man,' Tod will say later, commenting on the massacre.

The rest of the crew, it seems, finally realize what's going on, because they start shouting. a small Americano in a Borsalino (most of the others have taken off their cowboy hats, because of the wind), who could be the director, yells that he's going to call the police.

'Bastards! Don't shoot the chickens!' shouts the Americano.

One bullet whines in his direction ('This one's for you!') but the firing and shooting of the poultry stops.

Now both sides, each from its own end of the open space, are weighing each other up distrustfully.

An ominous silence hovers in the air, only the wind whines and sends an occasional plastic bag bowling along from the prairie. Crows sit on the black branches.

But, if we listen more closely, we can hear a rustle, then footsteps through the grass and a voice.

An unknown woman appears from behind the paddock, with plastic bags in her hands and, as far as can be made out, she seems to be calling a hen.

The gunslingers turn their heads towards the new arrival. They stare at the vision of a young woman with large yellow teeth.

When she notices them, she completely changes and smiles at them seductively. Totally deranged bitch, they think. Her skirt – Spanish style, with a floral pattern, is pulled up under her breasts, and she is wearing boots, with no heels. Under her shock of bleached white and yellow curls, two wild, enflamed green eyes gaze steadily at the men.

Then Čarija screams softly: she catches sight of the dirty white hen whose body, headless, is still twitching.

The aroma of a butcher's shop wafts on gusts of wind.

'Hey, here's Lily of the West come to see us, brother!' says the first gunslinger, apparently the group leader, judging by his stance.

Čarija spits a gob in his direction, which hits him in the face.

'Crazy bitch, damn you!' says the first gunslinger, loading his gun.

'Eeehaaah!' shouts another, cracking his whip in the air towards the girl. Maria jumps out of the way and growls. 'Eeehaaah, brother!' the man cracks his whip in the dust.

The men start laughing.

The woman drops her bag in alarm and its contents spill out. Then she runs a few metres, stops in the middle of the field and – not taking her eyes off her enemy – with her fingers spread she pats her open mouth several times briefly and jerkily: 'Va-va-va-va...'

And speeds to the hill, more swiftly than a vixen.

'Oh, brother, that's some crazy bitch,' says gunslinger number three. He blows at his trigger, takes aim and shoots off the head of a crow attracted by the smell of fresh hen's blood.

But where have Ned and Tod got to?

Just here, the road their pick-up is travelling on abruptly changes from four lanes to two. The speed limit is sixty, but everyone drives at least eighty, if not a hundred kilometres an hour: drivers here usually lose all sense of speed. Sometimes, at precisely this place, from one of the unmade-up side-tracks, a farmer in a tractor comes onto the highway, slowing the traffic completely, virtually stopping it.

So Ned and Tod, driving behind a tractor, can see through the washed windows of the truck an azure strip of sea and the chimney of the cement factory on the left and a poster in front of the Pastoral Centre, with *Jesus Loves You* on it on the right, and a traffic policeman watching out for drivers behind the discount store and two stray dogs passing beneath the newly washed larger-than-life General Gotovina, one behind the other, along the narrow dusty track beside the highway and turning off along the concrete stream-bed near the new buildings for war veterans and there disappearing from view.

'Oh man, have you ever seen a dump like this?' says Tod, peeling the wrapping from a Snickers bar.

'I'll tell you this, my friend, I've been in Europe and Africa and Australia, in Russia, both Americas, not to mention Austria and Hungary, Slovakia... I've been on the Slovene border and in Tirana. I've been in damn Santa Cruz on the island of Tenerife, in Rwanda and Niš, on the Ivory Coast, in Georgia and Columbia, but I have never ever seen such a shitty suburb as this,' says Ned.

'Aren't you from somewhere round here on you mother's side, man?' asks Tod.

'Oh yeah, maybe. But maybe not. You know, I'm more and more inclined to think not,' Ned smiles and swallows a swig of beer.

'Anyway, Tod, aren't you from Gilroy, the smelliest town in California, best known for its diabolical garlic ice-cream?'

'That's right, Ned,' Tod grimaces.

'You'll see, up there on the hill there's a quarry, grass and wilderness, better than Almeria for filming. The colours are sharper, everything's more intense. And, let's not ignore this item, Ned – it's fucking cheaper.'

Between the asphalt on one side and the brambles, groundsel and un-plastered houses on the other side of an imagined pavement, the wind raises dust, blows dry uprooted shrubs and trash about. Here – behind yet another petrol station and a few inns where suckling-pigs turn non-stop on a spit – Ned's pick-up, following a road-sign, turns off towards a local cemetery, and then, if they're thinking of reaching their destination, they ought to continue across the railway line along tarmac through the olive groves in the prairie.

Let's wish them a safe journey, because we leave the road here and climb up a goat track for a hundred metres or so up onto a hill. In front of us is a former slaughterhouse, behind the slaughterhouse is a copse, and in it a field chapel. From this spot, there is a magnificent view of the channel, the sea and the Old Settlement, but also of the nearby quarry that has served as a rubbish tip for years.

Just where the quarry ends is where there begin to rise up what are ugly buildings even for this part of the world: this is Majurina, the country estate, the ranch, tenure, small-holding of the old railway-track tribe – the relatives of the Iroquois Brothers.

The woman kicking the rotten gate in the fence and breaking into the scene is Maria.

Fortunately, her pa is behind the house, sheltered from the wind, feeling blue heads of cabbages with his black hands and choosing a large one for lunch.

Had he seen the way his daughter came in, the old man would have knocked her to the ground, silently, with a single blow to her back or belly. Then she would have grabbed him – as she had done before now– by his bony calf and bitten into it, dragging him down, lower, towards herself, scratching his face with her nails and whispering: 'I'll do you in, pa,' and then – because this is what he did for lesser offences – her father would throw a stone at her, or bash her with a tin bowl or spade, whatever was to hand. He would hitch up his trousers and spit beside the *snake*. He'd leave her on the ground, writhing, and say: 'You got what was coming to you.'

Had it been like that, and fortunately it wasn't, Tomi's triplets would have climbed onto the bare branches of the almond tree on the other side of the wire fence, three leggy girls with snotty noses, and, treating themselves to bread and Nutella or meat paste, they would have watched the contest as though it was a game of chess.

When she was thirteen, Maria Čarija had tried to batter her father with a hoe, it was a famous incident in the Old Settlement after which her pa shoved her into a cement mixer. Tomi had pulled her out alive and as enraged as a pagan she-devil.

Tomi Iroquois had warned his uncle not to touch his cousin, so people in the Settlement said.

People also said that mad Maria and her old man ate together, but that from that day on they both slept with knives under their pillows.

Unfortunately, we don't have time to peer into their pigsties and check what's hidden under their pillows, because time is flying, not standing still, and more important things are happening outside.

And nor do we have any reason not to believe Tomi Iroquois when he says that Maria doesn't need a cold weapon – she's too good a shot to dirty her hands.

So, while Maria's irascible and tousled pa is stepping between the beds of kale and endives, she kicks down the gate in the fence, enters the garden and then the house, where she finds a key with which, hurriedly, before the old codger appears, she opens the cellar door and vanishes into the darkness.

After a while, she appears in the cellar doorway, turns the key in the padlock and emerges into the light: merciless as the sun, sharp as the wind, but silent as the prairie and armed to the teeth.

She speeds, fierce and frowning, through the undergrowth, rushing through the impenetrable broom bushes, slipping down to the railway track where she cuts across the path of a pick-up and some baldie with a cigar yells at her in English.

148

She stares at him dumbfounded. Perhaps she's never seen anyone like him before.

As they pass, he shows her his middle finger.

Without hesitating, Maria takes out her daddy's pistol and aims at the passenger's rear-view mirror. BANG! BANG!

The other one, the driver, leaps off his seat.

'Holy shit, Tod!' He mutters between his teeth and puts his foot hard down. Stones scatter under the tyres into the air.

The girl spits and lowers her weapon, then takes off downhill.

The day is waning and the storm subsiding. Now the light is already softer and the plants are turning their stalks towards the west, while a swift, invisible animal bends the burned grass.

Hey, Maria Čarija, where have you set off to with that rifle, crazy lady from the railway track, you who aim at a bird's eye in flight?

What did Maria find in the cellar?

In the potato store, the Iroquois' old hiding place, she found: a Glock, a Beretta 92F, an Uzi and two hunting rifles, a Kalashnikov, three Thompsons and a hand grenade; The average arsenal of a railway-track house.

She selected a Winchester with a nice wooden butt, her pa's favourite – because it's elegant, because it's reliable, because it cocks easily and lies best in her hand. She stuffed cartridges and smoke bombs into her pockets.

Legend has it that someone in China dropped saltpetre into a fire and the flame began to spatter like a pyrotechnic fountain. And then Marco Polo brought that toy to the Old Continent. That's what Daniel, Rusty's late brother, told the Iroquois, but, nonetheless, who would have believed him, apart from Maria, when no one they knew had been able to make a firework out of saltpetre, just gunpowder for homemade bombs and smoke.

When he was alive, Maria's relations had called Daniel 'Cornboy', because his hair was neither black nor blond nor brown nor grey, but she had followed him, secretly, she couldn't stop pursuing him, there was nothing to be done – he was like a magnet.

One long-legged one with a thin moustache who looks like Lee Van Cleef and the other with the expression of a truly upright fellow and ulcer patient like that of Gary Cooper, have planted themselves, legs apart, in the middle of the prairie. They survey the scene in all directions in a macho way, then, like two bulls, they fly at one another and grab each other in a firm hold.

Van Cleef whacks Cooper, who gives as good as he gets. They clobber one another, draw back, gnash their teeth and waving their hands, they throw themselves on the earth, dust and scattered straw.

Feathers, straw, dust and hats – fly through the air.

Cooper gets to his feet, staggers slightly, raises his hand and misses Lee. But Van Cleef nevertheless smashes into a log and gets a mouthful of earth. He wipes his bloody nose with his sleeve and, seeing the blood, goes berserk.

'You see, Tod, that would never happen in a real Western,' says Ned. 'The ones who look like damn Lee, they never fight, they're too well-bred for that, and they're too good a shot to get their hands dirty.'

At that Van Cleef's double hurls himself furiously at the fake Cooper, striking sparks from the dust. Their wet neckerchiefs stick to their bare chests, while drops of sweat break out on their high tanned foreheads. As the cowboys roll and groan and scratch, the horses neigh in terror and one runs off – who knows where.

A quasi Grace Kelly, whom, according to the screenplay, all the men address as 'hey, gorgeous' or 'hello, sweetheart' approaches her window several times in panic and each time brings her little hand to her lips in horror.

And then Gary takes out his pistol: BANG! And the director in a panama hat, shouts: 'CUT!'

'You see, Tod, that would never happen in a real Western,' says Ned. 'The ones who look like good old Gary hit their mark infallibly, but they never, ever draw first.'

What else did Maria find in the cellar?

Sugar and saltpetre.

'This is a rather more complicated smoke bomb,' squad leader Dujković, a friend of Tomi Iroquois, had said once long ago, while the war was still on, 'but it can be made in larger quantities.'

The Iroquois Brothers, all nine male relations plus Maria Čarija, had arranged themselves on the settee and the floor, watching, while Dujković stood in the middle of the kitchen, stirring:

'All we need is saltpetre (potassium nitrate, KNO_3) and powdered sugar. You can buy saltpetre in any chemist's, 10 grams for 3 kunas, and sugar isn't a problem. We can buy larger quantities of saltpetre for fertilizer in a shop in Trogir, 2 kilos, but it's less pure so I don't know if it would work in this combination. The proportions of saltpetre to sugar are 3 to 2. So you take 3 grams of saltpetre and 2 of sugar. Take that and put it into a shallow metal pan, where you can mix it easily. Now turn the cooker ring to medium, perhaps a little higher, but not too high, and place the pan on it. In the meantime, while the ring is heating up (don't do this with gas, as the temperature is too high and it might set fire to the kitchen, as happened to me once), mix the saltpetre and powdered sugar, put it into the pan and keep stirring. Gradually a sticky mass will form, eventually becoming coffee-coloured. When that happens, take your freshly made smoke bomb off the heat and form it into whatever shape you like. To test it, set light to a small quantity with a lighter... there, there! It's smoking, see! Ammonia nitrate is a wickedly insensitive explosive. It's more likely that your pillow would explode than AN. It becomes sensitive in combination with liquid explosives, and can be detonated by quite a weak detonator. This is how I get a proper explosion: buy KAN fertilizer or fluorine or pinch it from your uncle's cellar '

Rumour had it that Dujković was a little mad and that he had gone to pieces over a Serbian girl, when her parents left for Belgrade, overnight, taking her away.

Dujković later told everyone prepared or obliged to listen to him, including the Iroquois Brothers, that the 'runaway had screwed with him at fourteen'. When he got drunk, he would yell that he'd 'make that little Serbian bitch pay' when he found her. He joined the Home Guard before he was eighteen and at nineteen he trod on a booby trap. They say that one day he simply ran into a minefield.

The girl came to look for him some years later. When she couldn't find him, she sat down on the steps of her former house and stayed there for eight hours. She never came back after that.

Maria had seen them, she wasn't the only one chasing Daniel – they were hunting him like hounds after a fox.

They had brought a little girl with them, sister of Ear and that new kid who had recently moved to the Settlement.

A Rottweiler known as Tiny, who ended up with a bullet in his back, and red-haired Daniel were standing, legs apart, in the middle of an empty car park, measuring each other up in a macho way. Then they launched themselves at one another and got a good hold. Tiny swung at Daniel who gave as good as he got. They laid into each other, snorting and waving their arms, they threw themselves down on the asphalt and sand and the flowerbeds round the streetlights. Daniel got up, staggered and missed Tiny. But Tiny still crashed over a step and got a mouthful of earth, he wiped his bloody nose with his sleeve and spat, and – seeing the blood – went berserk. And he threw himself at Daniel and everything exploded. Daniel grabbed his jacket and hurled him onto the ground. And then Ear, a mad terrier, Tiny's mate, whacked Daniel on the neck with a piece of board. Tiny growled and drew out his infamous long flick knife, snapping it open.

Daniel stepped back between the parked trucks and drew his pistol, braced himself, stretched out his arms and aimed at them.

But everyone in the Settlement knew that this pistol didn't work. Maria knew too. They knew about it in town, and at school, about the boy who carried a dud pistol.

There was a silence, then laughter, and guffaws.

And then, quite unexpectedly, Daniel fell. No one had touched him; he simply collapsed onto the ground. Tiny kicked him, hit him, put his knife under his chin, but Daniel didn't stir.

When he began to groan, they started kicking him in the thighs, arms and neck.

'That's enough. Come on, Ear, enough, you'll kill him,' said Ear's sister.

'Don't hit him in the head, I'm not getting banged up because of that cunt,' said Ear to Tiny.

'You're a real coward, Cornboy, you fainted like a proper piece of skirt,' said Tiny to Daniel.

They moved away for a while, muttering, then finally undid their flies and pissed on him. You've got to do that, it's classic. They took what he had in his pockets, and tossed the pistol towards the rubbish.

The new guy, the one with the mouth organ who used to hang around with them at that time, didn't touch Daniel, he stood to one side with his hands in his pockets, he looked round as he left, but he didn't go back.

Maria waited till the sons of bitches had moved sufficiently far away, pushed her way between the trucks and crawled up to Daniel.

He opened his eyes and sniffed his clothes, touched his head where it had hit the asphalt.

She watched him and as he didn't say anything, not even scram, she put his pistol in his hand and lay down beside him.

It was cold on the ground, but he didn't say get lost, as he sometimes did.

He just gazed at the moving clouds and the bright glare of the sun between them. She knew, because she was gazing at them too.

It was cold on the ground, but still – this time, she could have stayed there till morning.

Later she made little bombs just for him, for self-defence, they looked like the Albanian sweet-makers' rum-bombs, two and a half kunas each; but she never got round to giving them to him.

Whenever he sets off to the cowboys, to his first film job, Angelo, maestro on the mouth organ, doesn't walk along the road, he takes a roundabout route, through fields and vineyards, then over the railway track, through the undergrowth and tall grass, avoiding the streams overgrown with thorn bushes in which children and asparagus pickers sometimes find the washed and gnawed bones of dead animals and people, left over from several earlier wars which had rumbled through this transitional port of history and geography, somehow incidentally, in passing – leaving behind a lot of waste, desolation, filth and hysteria. This young man, you will observe from the way he moves, like a high-wire dancer, is taking care not to tear his tuxedo, not to dirty his trousers, not to catch himself on a cherry branch as he treads along the dry stone walls that stretch infinitely in four directions.

When the women picking olives, with their olive eyes and olive skins, catch sight of this freshly shorn head out of an anatomical atlas, moving above the bushes, they feel like holding it in their laps or at least passing their open hands over the short haircut – the younger ones put their fingers in their mouths and whistle.

Malicious people say that Angelo is a gigolo, but he is not a mannequin from a catwalk, a talking dildo, a toy-boy for women tourists, today he is, take a good look – the prince of the flatlands.

He always keeps to himself, in company he is usually silent, unless someone asks him something, but everyone agrees that he has presence, everyone pats him on the back and gladly treats him to a whisky in the bar of the *La Vida Loca* restaurant or a beer in the *Last Chance*.

He is a serial lover, a troubadour and adornment of the world, a being harmless as a butterfly, a sweet birdbrain with firm limbs, fragrant consolation for any girl who needs it.

Not intending any good, let alone harm, he used an ice-cream spoon to scoop out the hearts of wise virgins, and made the foolish a little more sensible. They opened their wallets, their legs, and their mouths and later accused the young man of having a stopwatch instead of a heart.

But today it's different, today he's the prince of the flatlands, as he steps through the fields in his blue tuxedo, he sheds the invisible jewellery that his lovers have hung round his neck, the bangles they clasped round his wrists; the wind has aired the scent of women's armpits and heavy perfumes from his clothes, cleared away the spit, tears, liquid powder, lubricants with banana extract and the sourness of vulvas from his skin.

He's young enough that it's still possible for an ordinary morning shower to wash him clean.

He forgets the exclamations of joy and screams, the contractions of thighs, the hot breath on his neck and the sobbing, the silver and pink vibrators, the brown, pinkish and blond clitorises, the stickiness of two bodies colliding and the touching battle of women to reach orgasm and 'love me, please' and 'come on, please' and all in vain.

He forgets the game as though he had switched off a porn film on the monitor and washed his dick in lavender.

As soon as he showers, shaves, puts on a clean T-shirt, the women and girls evaporate, with their moaning and weeping, and he finds their tears obnoxious.

He fantasizes about a great career and a great love.

That's why he's striding along like a cockerel, look at him, full of himself, audacious.

And now he's already near the bridge.

Out of superstition, he never comes this way, unless he has to – it was here that Daniel, Rusty's brother, threw himself under a train.

Whenever she goes to the cowboys, Maria doesn't go across the prairie, over the fields, she scampers round the other way, over the railway track, through the undergrowth, avoiding the streams overgrown with brambles, agaves and the thorns of wild roses in which children sometimes find the bones of dead occupiers. She tears her skirt with her fingers if it gets in her way, if it prevents her from stepping over a dry stone wall or jumping a fence.

She's not a mountain nymph from one of her pa's folk poems, but a dragon.

After she passes under the bridge, from whose concrete vault dirty slime drips as from a wound, she turns to see the rock from which Daniel, Rusty's late brother, is watching her.

Her relations called him Cornboy, but she was drawn to him as to a flame.

At one time, whenever she caught sight of him on the rock, she would quickly arrange her hair, caress her breasts, rub between her legs, purse her lips and smirk at him.

Or she would yell at him at the top of her voice.

Or else she would squat and rock on her heels, her head between her knees.

Daniel died in his eighteenth year, jumping from that bridge under an express train.

She had looked for him in vain the whole of the preceding evening and a good part of that day. She found the place in the crushed grass where he had lain, damp with hoar frost, and traces of the blood that had gushed out of his torn and broken limbs, through his nose and mouth.

She sat there until some inquisitive railway-track children appeared. Then she took herself off home with Daniel's school bag on her shoulder. She had found it in the tunnel under the highway, and now it was hers. It was hers, wasn't it?

Mathematics 4; *L'Italiano per Lei*; a sandwich, which she immediately ate, and a propelling pencil.

Maria often climbs onto the bridge and looks at the Settlement that is swallowing the golden grass, the olive groves clambering up into the bare hills and the seagulls flying in from the rubbish dump and from the direction of the slaughterhouse; the vineyards sprayed with Bordeaux mixture, poisonous and a childish colour, in which dark grapes grow, and dog-rose bushes full of hips and thorns.

They had run across this railway track countless times. The track was the frontier in times of war, just this place beside the bridge, where the St Andrew's cross is, and trains whistle as they pass. They were short battles; ambush attacks.

In the times of peace and privilege brought by good weather, together with their enemies, her Iroquois relatives stole bitter cherries in the fields and searched round the pylon for telephone wires which they would use to make bullets for their catapults. Or else they lowered themselves down into the cave, a closed quarry that served as an illegal rubbish dump, and there they found foreign newspapers with smooth shiny pages and gala adverts. That's how the afternoons usually passed.

They laid their ears on the tracks and listened to hear whether a train was coming.

Daniel always stayed longest, until the sirens went, until sparks started to leap on the rails from the train's brakes.

The other boys didn't let Maria onto the track.

Daniel sometimes told her to get lost, but sometimes let her come near.

Maria lays her head on the track: on her ear and temple she feels ice or red-hot metal, depending on the season and the time of day.

This is the time of impending death, soon the plants will wither and the bumblebees and other insects are already turning onto their backs as they fly.

She listens to the underground shifting beneath the surface of the soil – down there nothing has changed. Under the earth there is abundant life and death: tubers and bulbs turn into humus and a mole scratches under its crisp crust, ants grind grains of red soil into friable granules, and in the deeper layers fat white worms munch the hearts of the dead, an underground stream bursts its way through the clay, in the dense, saturated darkness silver and gold veins explode, minerals crackle, mandrake roots scream, while dead occupiers rearrange their bones.

Everything that falls onto the earth becomes nourishment, which someone on the underside of the pavement reheats, melts and sucks up through little straws.

If you don't believe this, ask yourself where all those fruits and large or small animal corpses, which no one collects or buries, disappear.

And if you still don't believe it – leave a dead dog in a field and in sixty days you will find only a dry tail. That's why Maria listens and never lies on the earth for long.

Out of superstition, Angelo never passes underneath the bridge, unless he really has to, he avoids it. Daniel, Rusty's brother, threw himself under a train there. The boy was a depressive, fuck him, thinks Angelo.

Since then, many of his former mates with whom he had plundered the highroads the year he returned to the Settlement from America had perished: Ear, Tiny, and the younger Barić. The whole secondary-school gang is now rotting under the black earth. Including Daniel, who had once been part of their team, until they began to chase him through the town.

He hadn't known Daniel well, and he doesn't remember whether they ever exchanged a word. And he doesn't know why they laid into him, he never asked. They beat up plenty of others, too. Sometimes they'd dream up a reason, sometimes they were just bored. Nothing particular. Mostly boredom. a reason is easily found.

And if the wolf doesn't have a cap, the bear clobbers him, while the rabbit cheers. If he does have a cap, same thing.

When Daniel killed himself, everyone said they were sorry. Everyone, apart from Angelo, went to the funeral: Tiny and Ear. Fuck it, the boy was a depressive, they said, which was shitty of them. If he hadn't killed himself, maybe they would have done it, who knows, Angelo thinks.

That time when they had run into Daniel in the empty car park and hammered him, he had turned round to check whether Daniel was alive.

He hadn't stopped, as he wasn't crazy, if you weren't with them, with Tiny and Ear, you'd be the next to be crying, pissed on, in the street. The whole town knew that. Apparently.

Angelo shakes the doubt from his heart as easily as a puppy shakes off dirty water.

He's still young enough for ordinary shower gel to be able to wash him clean and the wind to dry him, he thinks.

That's why he sails like a harvest moon, full of himself.

He doesn't pause until, from the top, he catches sight of a colourful apparition moving in the distance in the same direction as him.

At the same time, just a few minutes' walk away:

What the devil was that dotard Ned up to now? thought Tod.

He had been holed up in that chemical toilet for twenty minutes.

If Tod had had his way, those idiots who had carried out the massacre of the fowl would by now have been in a police car on

159

their way to their idiot village, which like all idiot villages in this world no doubt prides itself on its idiocy.

But Ned, oh yes, that guy never for an instant forgets that he is Ned Montgomery, man. He had swayed up to the gunslinger from B, like a cowboy, with a cigar in his mouth, and said: 'Save the damn bullets, boys.'

That was how Tod's teacher, in Gilroy, California, would have confiscated the kids' water pistols till the end of the lesson, thought Tod.

And what a spectacular final showdown, man, why this isn't Hollywood, for God's sake, give me a break, amigo. Let's go, finally, finish the job and pick up our dosh.

'Hey, Ned, you OK, old man?' Tod knocks on the door of the chemical toilet. 'D'you think you could get a bit of a move on?'

(Swearing from inside.)

The door opens and Ned comes out, in clean clothes.

'Surprise,' says Ned.

'Hee, hee,' he says. 'I'm going to shoot in the damn final showdown too,' he says. He takes two golden Colts, of the six he has, out from under his leather coat, real buffalo skin, and spins them on his fingers. An old trick, Ned Montgomery never needed a double.

I've never understood what in hell's name he needs with those six pistols, man, he's not Shiva! thinks Tod.

Hell, Ned, that's not in the screenplay, he starts to say, but his cigar singes him.

Mr Montgomery, that's not in the screenplay, the Americano director starts to say, but concludes that it's not advisable and there's no point in protesting.

'Let's go, lads,' says Montgomery, tilting his hat. 'Let's go film! Drag yourselves over to me here, since I've dragged my magnificent butt over the Ocean to you. It's time for a real goddam turbo Western party.'

'Oh, man.'

We left Angelo sailing like a full moon, above the olive groves and stopping, for a moment, when he catches sight from the hilltop of a figure a bit further off stirring up dust in the same direction as himself. He recognizes Tomi Iroquois's relation, the one who hisses at him when they meet on the road, so he slows down, letting that crazy woman move as far ahead as possible.

Today the charmer Angelo believes that he's happy, because he thinks he's in love with Rusty, the girl who, at this moment, on the other side of town, is getting onto a train and leaving him.

But, he knows nothing of that, he takes his harmonica, his Pocket Pal, out of his pocket, spreads his palm and his hand opens into a peacock's tail, while his lips become a starling's beak. He weaves tunes, a little sweet, and a little sad. In his head he is Sugar Blue.

He dreams about a great career as a musician, and he thinks about an ordinary, true love.

He believed that love was big and clear, but real and tangible, like a monolith, which is a fairly ignorant notion. Now that he's inside it, he can see a bit – it's a moist box containing two blind hungry greedy kittens. There's no way out and nothing else exists.

You wanted to tell her things about yourself, sweet Angelo, while you lay naked and completely exposed like really small children, your limbs intertwined in the chilly cellar room.

But you didn't, that's how it turned out, she fell asleep or you fell asleep. In short, you put your snout into her ear and mumbled: 'Sleep, Rusty.'

She'll be your best friend, your *fratella*, your favourite lover, you convince yourself, after just a few days, pressed into those few hours of intimate contact – and your wife.

You really believe that you're in love with that gangling, rusty girl who is just leaving town, while you, fool, have no clue.

In that unrepeatable second being counted out by your fast, unaccountable heart, you defy the wind, more boldly than the fleeting Kairos and you believe that you are stronger than everything that has lain in store for you so far. Like – the story is about to take a new direction.

And it is, but not exactly the way you hope, sweet Angelo.

Do you not know that it's your fault your rusty bride has just taken her seat in the train and is leaving you?

Be careful, because this will be a bad day even for people with better luck.

They fired, she crumpled.

She had crept up, stepped out in front of the camera and yelled: 'Now you're going to pay for your sins!'

All the actor cowboys stopped with their *Airsoft* responses in their hands.

One shouts: 'Lily's back, brother! She liked it.'

And he fires rata -tat -at -atat in her direction. Some others join him. They laugh. Good joke.

'Are you crazy?!' someone shouts.

'Scram, out of my sight!' he shouts, from behind the container. 'Call the police!'

Maria thinks-those are real rifles and pistols, they're shooting at her.

Fucking cretins, fucking cretins, they're shooting at her.

She's cut her lip and her blouse is filthy. She throws two smoke bombs, nimbly, like a real railway track savage, rolls back, behind the horse's paddock, aims between the feet of some of the enemies and fires. Her Winchester isn't a model; her bullets are real. Maria Čarija can hit the eye of a bird in flight, if only she wants to.

The cowboys all shit themselves, they scamper behind barrels, props, horses, anything. Some fly headfirst into brambles, not caring, running for their lives.

Fucking cretins, now dare to shoot.

'Throw down your weapons, in Christ's name!' shouted the man in the long leather coat she had seen half an hour earlier in the pickup. 'All of you!'

He has stepped into the middle of the flatland with his arms raised – he is standing in the line of fire. He throws down one by one, all six of his golden pistols, so that Maria sees. Beside him,

Maria observes, stands a man with a camera, also with his hands up, and that guy who looks like a bearded, bald woman, from the pickup, who showed her his finger. He's crying.

Maria holds her rifle against her shoulder, her hand is still. She watches them – through the barrel – as they fill their pants.

'All put your hands up and come out!' shouts Maria. 'Someone's got to pay for this fuck-up! For my hen!'

Her eyes are almost stuck together with crusts, her face is dirty and her lip stings. She has only one boot on her foot, and that's only half on. She drags it after her. No one stirs. And the wind has dropped.

A crow says: Caw. It flutters to another tree and repeats: Caw.

Through a curtain of smoke, onto the stage steps Angelo.

He stops in the middle of it all, not understanding what's going on. Is this a film? Who's doing the shooting?

'What's this? Is it the film?' asks Angelo.

In the midst of the silence his voice cracks as though thrown into a well.

Čarija gives a start, turns her rifle towards him for a moment, measuring him up with contempt. He's not dangerous, thinks Maria. He's chicken shit, he's standing aside.

And she aims the rifle barrel at that dubious trio with their hands in the air.

The woman who makes the coffee for the film crew had crouched down and covered her head with her jacket. She could be heard calling for help under her breath. Caw. Caw.

But when Maria Čarija turned her gun away, Angelo had quickly reached his hand into his pocket.

She aims, quickly, and hits him in the hand.

Immediately, as though it had been waiting for an excuse to be fired, someone's bullet, a real bullet, hits her. Then another.

Maria looks at Angelo in surprise. She fires again and hits him in the chest.

Angelo looks at Maria in surprise, collapses.

They fired for about half a minute, Maria Čarija, they fired 14 bullets into you, 10 of them into your poor head. At firing ranges the head carries most points, maybe that's the explanation.

Now you're lying motionless, you and Angelo, as though you're playing dead. He with a hole in his chest, you, your face shattered, with no eyes.

Your eyes don't sting any more. Nothing hurts you any more, Iroquois sister.

You don't hear the buzzing of the horse flies. You don't see that people have started approaching, sweating, dismayed, unbelieving.

'Death is certain, only its moment is uncertain,' said a Tibetan this morning on the TV. By chance, like. Just this morning, while Angelo was putting on his socks and cleaning his teeth, like every morning.

Maybe it was the Dalai Lama thinks Angelo as he lies, shot.

What would the Dalai Lama say about Daniel, then? That he took matters into his own hands?

What a stupid random event, Angelo thinks as he lies, shot, and tries to feel with his fingers in the dust for his mouth organ. But it's hard for his fingers to move; they'll need several more springs before they sprout out of the grass and reach the instrument.

He had only wanted to put his instrument back in his pocket. Why on earth had she shot him?

The smoke cleared above the young man and the heads of men in cowboy hats approached.

'This is, probably, not hell, but it certainly isn't paradise,' Angelo would say, if he could, as he lies with the hot metal in his flesh, and his bright red blood grows and steams on the cooling ground. Under the earth the dead occupiers are already getting out their little straws for the juice.

The world is an uncertain place. But before that uncertain place drips away through a dark speck, which is perhaps just a splinter in his eyes, Angelo sees another figure standing over him and recognizes the cowboy from the poster hanging in Rusty's little room. As though he has come down from the wall: he's wearing that same brown leather coat and the boots with the gleaming spurs, real gold.

He leans towards Angelo and stops his blood with his hands.

'God dammit,' says the great cowboy from the poster.

Hey, the real Ned Montgomery thinks Angelo. Why, this is brilliant. Let this be the last thing. a speck.

THE END

Farewell

My sister leaves me at the junction, at the railway station that looks like the end of the world. It's the last station, the end of the journey. It looks deserted even when there are people about.

'Off you go then, I've got work to do,' says my sister, waiting just long enough for me to take my case out of the boot, and then her car disappears. She just winked, she didn't hug me and I didn't need to say anything along the lines of take care of yourself, take care of Ma or any of the other things I'd been rehearsing in my head on our way here.

The junction is behind the abandoned halls of the former fish processing factory, which everyone calls the Sardine Factory and which has served for years mainly as a squat – until the police come and throw the squatters out, and then it becomes yet another shit-house and refuge for the most desperate dope-heads. At the entrance there's a half eligible graffito: **LOVE HURTS LIKE A RASP RUNNING OVER…**

The former Sardine Factory building is not high, but it's the only protection against the wind between the Railway Station and the warehouses of the industrial port. Cargo ships, water tankers and tugs fray their ropes. Tugs are, along with towboats, the nicest boats in the world, I reflect: Little musclemen with big names on their prows and a piece of car tyre instead of a protégé. Tugs with rough thick paint in bright colours, green, orange, on a steel hull – they are definitely the nicest boats in the world, although in principle, and even with none, I would have no objection to being shat on by some bird and sailing off on a yacht.

The wind swirls weed from the shore, so there is dried seaweed and sea salad all over the junction – and on the rails.

I'm the last person to get onto the train, at the last minute.

'You do everything by the skin of your teeth, Dada,' my room-mate would say. a cheery emo lass. She'll be waiting for me tomorrow at the Munich Hauptbahnhof. For us to cook tortillas together, for our legs to swell up from standing too much and for us to go out into the streets clattering our little boots in a harmonious rhythm, while around us stretches one of the centres of the universe, which we wouldn't be able to traverse even if we had a hundred days.

'There's nowhere to escape to,' said Herr Professor, once, I recall, maybe in the letter he left me or in a conversation, I can't remember now, but it was about journeys, departures and the like.

But it's not about escaping, Professor, I tell him to myself, you're the one escaping, I'm done here and it's time for me to ride off into the sunset.

There's a woman with dark hair sitting in my compartment, reading a newspaper. The way she responds to my greeting suggests that she's not pleased to be sharing those few cubic metres of stale air with me, a stranger. The seats are covered in artificial leather, with the stuffing spilling out in places where it's been pierced and scrawled over with ball-point pens, but the windowpanes are crystal clear.

Later, my travelling companion introduces herself: 'Mrs Nought, writer.'

On the seat beside her there's a bag for a laptop. She's put her feet onto her suitcase – black boots, with laces – and thrust her nose still more deeply into her newspaper.

She's no more agreeable than a corpse, I reflect, but nevertheless I don't think she'll take out the usual snack of meat, onion and brandy in the middle of the journey, and that's something. Although you can never be quite sure of these things in this part of the world.

The engine whistles.

On our way out of town I see a crowd of people, whole columns. They're railway workers, on strike.

'Someone's on strike every day,' said Ma in hospital.

She's bored, but she hates watching programmes in the TV room 'with those lunatics', as she calls them. 'They stink.' So she reads all the newspapers that Mariana Mateljan brings her. She is most interested in the people on hunger strike. 'They're going to die,' she said, shaking her head. But none of the strikers died, and the journalists would soon forget them and then new ones would appear, and so it went on.

There are lots of workers in the street, they look as though they don't know where to go: I see them through the train window, men and women. They're not so much carrying their placards as dragging them along.

No one shouts or bursts into song like in the old text books.

The engine driver has to slow down and whistle, because some of the workers are strolling across the track as though they weren't remotely concerned about the train. In the end, the train stops before we've even properly got going.

It looks as though we're being driven by strikebreakers.

The woman in the compartment doesn't notice what's going on or else she pretends not to; she's taken off her black leather jacket and made herself comfortable as she carries on reading. On the front page of the tabloid she has in her hands it says 'Strike...' and something else hidden by her fingers.

She looks only a few years older than me, but there's something about Mrs 0 that would make even older people prefer to remain on formal terms with her.

'Do you like trains?'

'Not particularly.'

'I like trains, regardless of the bad air. What precisely is it that you don't like about trains?'

'Someone close to me threw himself under one. So it'd be stupid for me to say I like trains. Otherwise I don't have anything against them.'

'I'm sorry. Now I feel awkward.'

'I understand, but there's no need.'

'Peter Pan threw himself under a train, as well, did you know? Peter Davis, actually, on whom Barrie based Peter Pan. He didn't fly, the poor flying boy – or flying granddad. He was already an old man up to his ears in debt. Although some say the fact that he killed himself had something to do with his brother Michael who had drowned very young, deliberately, out rowing with his boy-friend. Romeo and Romeo. Poor Peter, apparently, never got over it. Sometimes I wonder, hypothetically, whether it wouldn't have been better for poor Peter to have done it straight away, rather than wait all those years, for his wife and children to fall ill, to get into financial trouble and so on. In a word, for all those things to happen that it's virtually impossible to avoid.'

'A very sad story. a bit absurd.'

'It depends how you look at it. Are you very sad?'

'I was. I'm not sad now.'

'But you're not happy either?'

'No, I'm not happy, but I'm calm.'

'Can you explain?'

'The person I lost was my brother Daniel. I believed that we were very close, but he didn't ask for my help. It seems I didn't know him that well. Can one get over that, Mrs 0? Or does one just become dulled to an extent that's bearable. I went back to the Old Settlement in order to discover the truth about him.'

'And? Was the quest successful? Did you find the Holy Grail?'

'Well, I'm just trying to tell you, I found some of his letters and discovered that his heart was in the right place. Unfortunately, for a while I hadn't been sure of that. But there's no question, my brother wasn't selfish or bad. He was a fine boy. He could have become an astronomer or a poet, not everyone can do that.'

'What does *bad* mean for you?'

'That he wasn't bad? Treacherous or violent, he wasn't that. All vicious people are one or the other. One shouldn't have anything to do with such people. He was sound.'

'And is that some consolation?'

'Not really, is it, but it helps nevertheless. One day at a time.'

'What was your brother like?'

'Different. Everything about him was over the top. Too much fog in his head, our sister would say. It seems he wanted to be an astronomer, he knew a lot about stars, but one could also say he could have been a poet – but I didn't know that until a few days ago. What else. He had lots of animals and took care of them. On the other hand, he wasn't brilliant at everyday things. In school he

was slower than the others. His teachers said he didn't concentrate...
he played at being a cowboy. That's charming when you're nine,
but not really after that.'

'Like Shane?'

'Yes, like Alan Ladd, James Stewart, Gregory Peck, Kirk Douglas,
Charles Bronson, Burt Lancaster, Yul Brynner, Steve McQueen,
Gary Cooper, John Wayne, Clint Eastwood, James Coburn,
Terence Hill, Lee Marvin, Lee Van Cleef, Montgomery Clift, Ned
Montgomery.'

'You've got a good memory.'

'I like lists, they're amusing.'

'I'd completely forgotten about cowboys. Gold diggers, cattle
rustlers, and law keepers. Mythical fellows with honour, balls,
a swagger in their step. What posers, don't you think?!'

'Some just look like cowboys, but some really are.'

'A shame they've lost their point. Wonderful posers. How did you
put it? With their hearts in the right place, well centred.'

'Yes, and with balls. In the right place.'

'Do you know any?'

'Cowboys? They exist, for sure,' I say.

'Like life in space,' Mrs 0 smiles. 'Don't be cross,' she adds. 'I
believe in life in space.'

Suddenly she moves over to me. She sits down by my feet and
plays with her fingers.

'Have you other family?'

'I've got Ma and my sister.'

'How do you get on with them?'

'I want my sister and Ma to be happy and well, more than anything, but I can also live without them.'

'One day at a time, is that how you live?'

'That's one way. It can be one minute at a time, as well.'

'You mention your mother and sister. No one else. Don't you
have anyone else close to you? Aren't you in love, for instance?'

'No. But I've slept with several men and I cared for them then.'

'And now?'

'There was a young man I liked, but he turned out bad.'

'Bad in bed?'

'In bed we were one. That doesn't happen with everyone, I thought that meant something.'

'So, the young man is, how did you put it – vicious? Violent or treacherous?'

'He was in a group with violent people who mistreated my brother and he didn't tell me. He hurt me.'

'Treacherous, then? Is that why you're leaving?'

'That's just one of the reasons I didn't stay.'

'That's your revenge?'

'I don't know, I don't think so, I didn't have a choice. Revenge includes choice.'

'You know what they say: revenge is best served cold. It's not an empty phrase. But, if you ask me, it's also excellent hot. But you're tepid. Some would say – lukewarm. If you ask me you ought either to have stayed with him or killed him at once, as soon as you found out. Shoot him, and that's the end of it. Hypothetically: if his life depended on your word, would you take revenge or save him?'

I say nothing.

'You forget about the good side of death. Death redeems,' she adds.

'To be quite honest, I don't give a damn about the good side of death.'

'I thought as much,' says the writer 0 and smiles.

The police come and order the workers to get off the tracks and let the train through. a woman shouts, but soon the strikers withdraw, still carrying their placards at half-mast. Some have stuck theirs in rubbish bins. 'At least people used to be alarmed by them, but now no one gives a flying fuck,' my sister had said a few days earlier when the shipyards were on strike.

Mrs 0 keeps smiling and clicking her fingers.

'They're ignoring them,' says 0 as though she has suddenly noticed the people outside.

'What do you think's going to happen?' I ask.

'When they're hungry enough, they'll take up arms, then people will have to take notice. They'll be given some money or the angry will blow them to smithereens.'

'But there's no money in this country. My sister says that we've been robbed by our big-wigs and heroes.'

'Then they've got the money,' says Mrs 0.

The engine could be heard puffing like a sportsman before the start of a race.

'Have we met somewhere before?' I ask.

'No. People often ask me that. I seem familiar,' says 0.

She's blushing, I observe. You don't expect a person of such poise to blush.

I turn my head away and pretend to be watching the railway coming back to life, the strikers getting increasingly tiny and the views changing. I observe the town as though it's unfamiliar, and the more success I have with looking through the eyes of an unknown man or woman, the more alien the town is to me – the more I like it. The more I like it, the less I care about it. And the other way round.

'This town cannot be conquered in any familiar way, it is inherited like an illness,' said Herr Professor. 'That's what Vrdovđek and those like him cannot grasp,' he said. 'The town will devour their brain and soul, far more quickly than they will destroy it.'

I wouldn't be so sure, I reflect.

The train rumbles over the rocky ground. I shield my eyes from the sun with my hands so as to see the prairie in the distance, the infertile Majurina and the house of my old enemies and friends from my childhood, the Iroquois Brothers. And I look also, into the distance, so as not to miss the place where I had briefly, but fundamentally, fallen for Angelo. *Colpo di fulmine*, said my great-grandma *the insatiable one*. It lasts an instant and the picture is lost. We are emerging from the urban catacombs and before us the plane begins to stretch out, with its fields and trees, a few houses and the hill in the distance. Soon one can no longer see the suburbs, the Old Settlement, or the sea.

THE AUTHOR

OLJA SAVIČEVIĆ

Olja Savičević is a poet, writer and journalist from Split, Croatia. Having gained a degree in Croatian language and literature she worked as a teacher of creative writing. For the past ten years, she has been working as an independent writer and a columnist in newspapers and internet portals. Her first collection of poetry was published when she was only fourteen, and since then she has published six collections of poems, the short story collection "To make a dog laugh" (2006) and the novel "Farewell, Cowboy" (2010). Olja regularly collaborates with theatres as a dramatist and writes lyrics for theatre songs, and two of her short stories have been adapted into short films. The manuscript of "To make a dog laugh" won Olja the prize for the best prose author under thirty-five awarded jointly by *Vijenac*, a Croatian literary magazine, and the publishing house AGM. She is also the recipient of the *Ranko Marinković* award for the best short story in 2007 and the Kiklop prize for the best poetry collection in 2008. 'Farewell, Cowboy' was awarded the *Roman T-portal* best Croatian novel of 2011 and was adapted into a successful stage play the following year. An excerpt of the novel has been included in Dalkey Archive's *Best European Fiction 2014* and won her a place at the *International Writing Program at the University of Iowa*. Olja Savičević's work has been included in a number of Croatian anthologies and International selections, and her writing has been translated into over seventeen languages, including Zulu.

THE TRANSLATOR

CELIA HAWKESWORTH

Celia Hawkesworth taught Serbian and Croatian at the School of Slavonic and East European Studies, University College, London, 1971-2002. She has published numerous articles and several books on Serbian, Croatian, and Bosnian literature, including the studies *Ivo Andrić: Bridge between East and West* (Athlone Press, 1984); *Voices in the Shadows: Women and Verbal Art in Serbia and Bosnia* (CEU Press, 2000); and *Zagreb: A Cultural History* (Oxford University Press, 2007). Her translations of Dubravka Ugresić's *The Museum of Unconditional Surrender* was short-listed for the Weidenfeld Prize for Literary Translation, and *The Culture of Lies* won the Heldt Prize for Translation in 1999. .